MARSHAL OF SANGAREE

Ben Craig had a five-year-old message from his friend Chalco for the Luvain brothers—in the form of two bullets with their names on them.

The first day that Ben rode into the Sangaree Valley he delivered the first of those messages to Pete Luvain, but his brother Cloyd wasn't going to be easy. For one thing, Cloyd was too busy trying to take over the whole of Sangaree to handle any unfinished business. For another thing, Ben had to go easy on hunting his personal gun-troubles—as long as he had become responsible for law and order in the whole town. But they were bound to meet one day . . .

MARSHAL OF SANGAREE

Louis Trimble

GUNSMOKE

This hardback edition 2004
by BBC Audiobooks Ltd
by arrangement with
Golden West Literary Agency

ISBN 0 7540 8273 3

British Library Cataloguing in Publication Data available.

Printed and bound in Great Britain by
Antony Rowe Ltd., Chippenham, Wiltshire

MARSHAL OF SANGAREE

I

THE DAY had been hot for late September, and as Ben Craig walked his leggy paint horse up the steep slope to the summit of the pass, he was grateful for the sun's sliding down behind the Sangaree range to the west. By the time he topped the crest and started along the flat, he could feel the first faint whisper of a wind sliding out of Canada less than thirty miles to the north.

He thumbed back his hat to let the moving air dry the sweat on his forehead. One gloved hand reached out to pat the paint on the neck. "There's a little smell of Montana winter in that," he said.

The horse let a ripple run over his skin as if he already felt the chill of November. Craig patted him again and then straightened in the saddle, looking around at this new country and letting his mind work on what lay ahead for him.

The road here ran level across the top of the pass a full furlong before breaking down in a gentle slope to the floor of the Sangaree valley. At the end of the level stretch, Craig reined in and studied the sweep of land below—noticing the way the valley ran dry looking and straight and narrow up to where a river came out of the east hills, looped around

5

a sprawl of buildings, and then ran almost due north. Coming almost straight across from the west, where the Sangarees were outlined against the gold glow of the freshly set sun, a line of willows marked a creek running to meet the river. Beyond the point of their meeting, the dry look stopped, and even from this distance Craig could see the deeper green of well watered land running north to where the valley ended in a jumble of hills.

"Nice country," Craig told the paint. "And that town looks big enough to interest the Luvain brothers—or whatever they call themselves now."

His expression became bleak and he turned in the saddle, studying the small log roadhouse sitting in the middle of a cluster of tumbledown, abandoned corrals. Five horses tied to the hitching rail said that the place was open for business, and Craig wondered whether to take the time to rest here or to ride on to the town of Sangaree and settle in for the night before having his supper. Before, he added to himself, beginning his hunt for the Luvains.

He could feel the weariness of the paint from the day's long, hot ride. "It looks about three miles to town," he told the horse. "So let's have a quick stop and then move along."

He reined the paint up to the hitching rail and ran it alongside a deep-chested, fine looking black gelding and a blaze-faced sorrel mare. Automatically, he glanced at the brands as he dropped to the ground. Both horses carried PJ on their flanks. It was no brand Craig had ever heard of.

He walked around the mare, taking a look at the other three horses. Two were nondescript, worn-out looking, and carried no sign of ownership on their flanks. The third was a heavy, solid looking gray wearing a Diamond Bar. But it was the saddle rather than the brand that held Craig's attention.

It was a Spanish-type single rig with the cinch far forward, and the fork shallow. It wasn't a common saddle, and Craig could remember seeing at most half a dozen in his travels. Of those half dozen, two belonged to the Luvain brothers. But he had learned that too late, just as he had figured out too late that the Luvains changed their names a lot more often than they changed their shirts.

6

Craig shook his head. Saddles didn't mean much. Yet in the five years he had been hunting the Luvains, one of the threads that had helped him follow their tortuous trail had been the constant description of their saddles—in Texas, along the Rio Grande; in the mountains of northern New Mexico and southern Colorado; in the flat cattlelands of western Kansas and Nebraska; in the high country of Wyoming.

But there was only one Spanish rig, and the Luvains always traveled together. Craig shrugged at his own wishful thinking. He glanced down into the valley turning purplegray under the dying light. If the brothers weren't here, they would be down there somewhere. The old trapper at Fort Benton had been too accurate in his descriptions, too sure of his facts for Craig to doubt him. The Luvains had found reason to stay in this corner of Montana longer than they had stayed in any one place since Craig had begun hunting them.

So, Craig thought, it didn't matter if he found them now or tonight or next week. After five years, a little more waiting was nothing.

He moved slowly to the door of the roadhouse, a tall man, solid through the shoulders, with his expression tight and his smoky gray eyes ever watchful. His mouth had the thin, hard set of the dedicated man, but there remained in it the hint of a once easy smile, of an outgoing friendliness.

Craig opened the door and stepped into a room redolent of raw pine boards, of stale liquor, and of men who had ridden hard and long between baths. He stopped abruptly, letting the door ease shut behind him. There was none of the talk he had expected to hear from men who had stopped here to ease away a day's work with a glass of beer or whiskey. There was only thick silence.

The bar ran the width of the room and the barkeep behind it looked as if he wanted to lie down on the floor and hide himself. He stood with his back to the bottles lined up under the bar mirror, his hands held up and away from his sides. At the near end of the bar, holding to it with gloved hands clenched fiercely to the wood, was a lushly beautiful, dark-haired young woman. She was no saloon

7

girl, Craig saw, not with those expensively elegant riding clothes and not with her almost extravagantly patrician features.

Three men stood in front of the bar, and one leaned against its far end. He held a shotgun aimed loosely between the bartender and the woman and he grinned to show missing teeth in an unshaven face. He seemed to be enjoying himself.

Of the three men closer to Craig, two faced him and the third showed only a broad back and an arrogant set to his head. Craig's eyes absorbed the scene quickly—he had seen it often enough over the years. The man with his back to Craig was standing tensely, balanced so as to be able to move forward quickly. His gun rode in his holster, leaving his hands empty and hanging a little away from his sides. The nearest of the pair facing him was a well set up man, dressed in rancher's garb that matched the woman's clothes in quality and price. He was fine featured, with the barest hint of gray threading his moustache and goatee. The dark eyes staring from his tanned face held steadily on the man facing him, and they reflected nothing but contempt.

Yet, Craig thought, he should show some signs of fear. The lanky, meatless man behind him held a gun to his back so that he dared not risk going for the fancy looking weapon in his holster. And soon, Craig was sure, the broad-backed man would move forward and start using his fists. Because this had all the earmarks of a bully boy fight—where a man was made helpless and then had to stand and take his beating.

Without moving his body at all, the broad-backed man said, "Who came in, Shorty?"

The man with the shotgun kept on grinning. "Some stranger. But he don't seem eager to join in. He better not, unless he wants a load of my buckshot."

Craig scarcely heard Shorty. He was listening to the broad-backed man as he said in a soft, bayou country drawl, "If it's a friend of yours, Jerrod, tell him quick to step on up here. He can't do you no more good than Mrs. Jerrod over there can."

Craig moved to the side to give himself an angle view of the features of the broad-backed man. Now he could see

8

the chiseled features, the dark, curly hair showing under the edge of a thumbed-back hat. His breath jammed in his throat and his palms went damp with sweat. With an effort, he caught and held his control. He had never seen either of the Luvain brothers, but after five years, he had got a picture of them—their sharp, chiseled features, their arrogant way of holding themselves, of walking, and the soft bayou drawls they had never lost from their speech.

"You," Craig said, "what's your name?" He was surprised at the steadiness of his own voice.

The man made a half turn and let eyes the color of pale blue ice rake over Craig. "What difference does it make, stranger? Your friend Jerrod here's going to get a beating no matter what my name is."

"I never saw the man before," Jerrod said in a quick, assured voice. "Leave him out of this affair, Luvain."

If he had needed to hear the name to be sure, he had it now, Craig thought. A strange sensation of unreality gripped him. This was the beginning of the end—the last stretch of the long trail that had begun where he held Chalco's sun-battered body in his arms and felt death take away the last of the pain racking his friend.

Softly now, Craig said, "I don't know Mr. Jerrod. I didn't come here looking for him. I came to see you, Luvain. I've got a message—from Chalco."

"Me?" Luvains's heavy eyebrows lifted. "Chalco?"

"Chalco," Craig repeated in the same soft, steady voice. "A U.S. Cavalry scout down in the Arizona desert. You ran into him in the hot country west of Tuscon."

Luvain's expression was faintly puzzled. "Arizona? I ain't been there in years."

"Five years," Craig agreed. "The message is that old."

Luvain lost his interest. "I don't know your game, stranger, but move over where my boys can keep their eyes on you. And hold your hands where they can see them."

Craig ignored the order. "You knew Chalco," he said. "You and your brother stumbled on his camp when you were lost in the desert and dying of thirst. You ate his food and drank his water and the next morning you left him with a bullet-broken leg and a dying horse. When I found him

9

he was still alive, and within a quarter of a mile of a water-hole. He gave me a message. I've spent five years trying to deliver it."

Luvain's pale eyes widened and he stared at Craig in disbelief. "Five years! You mean you been hunting me and Cloyd for five years on account of that—that breed Indian?"

"That breed Indian was my friend," Craig said. "I promised him I'd kill you both."

Luvain's flat mouth split open and he laughed. Craig said, "I'm giving you more chance than you gave him." He held his hands well away from his sides. "Make your draw first."

Luvain laughed louder. "Hear that, boys. With two guns on him, he figures to kill me! To outshoot me and kill me!"

"In five years, I never heard of you or your brother fighting without the odds at least two to one in your favor," Craig said with thick contempt. "Now they're three to one—and you haven't got the belly to face me down."

Luvain cursed him, twisted around to Craig's direction and slapped his hand for the gun at his waist. Craig let him clear leather and then he moved. His gun was in his hand and blasting before Luvain could bring his barrel high enough to shoot. He took the lead full in the chest and went backward, his gun sending a bullet harmlessly into the ceiling and then clattering to the floor. His back slammed against the edge of the bar and he hung there a moment before sagging forward to lie crumpled on the dirty floor.

Craig kept on moving after he shot and now he sent a bullet chipping wood from the bar by Shorty. At the same instant, Jerrod dropped down and came around, sweeping the legs out from under the gunman behind him. As the man fell, Jerrod drove a vicious fist into his face, splitting his lip and sending blood streaming from his long, thin nose.

Shorty started to bring his shotgun around toward Craig and then let it drop, muzzle aimed at the floor. "Hold it, mister. Jenks and me didn't contract for no killing."

"Drop your gun," Craig ordered. The gun hit the floor. "Now move over against the back wall." Shorty moved quickly.

10

Craig turned his attention to the others. Jerrod was on his feet. The lanky man lay unmoving. Jerrod wiped his hands fastidiously on a handkerchief as he walked toward the woman. She had not moved but still clutched the edge of the bar as if frozen to it. Jerrod stepped over Luvain's prone body without so much as a glance downward.

"I'm sorry, my dear," he said soothingly to the woman. "Now relax. It's all over. This gentleman here—" He turned toward Craig. "You'll take a drink with us? We stopped to rest our horses and get my wife some water. But I think she needs something stronger right now."

"I think I'll ride to town and settle in before I have my supper-time drink," Craig said. He walked to Luvain and knelt. "He's dead," he announced to no one in particular.

The woman made a half choking sound. Jerrod said sharply, "Calm yourself, Anita! It's good enough riddance." His voice smoothed out and he turned a charm-heavy smile on Craig. "If you're riding to town, let me offer you the hospitality of the Sangaree House. I own it and I'd be honored to have you stay there." He came forward, his hand out. "I'm Park Jerrod."

Before Craig could rise and give his name, a sudden scrabbling turned both men toward the rear. They were in time to see Shorty and the lanky Jenks race out the back door.

Jerrod said quickly, "I'll see you at the hotel. My wife will escort you, I'm sure. Right now I seem to have some unfinished business."

He hurried out the front. As he disappeared, the woman spoke for the first time. "Park, watch out for Cloyd! He—" She broke off as the sound of three horses hammering away filled the air. Her shoulders sagged.

Craig rose and moved quickly toward her. "Barkeep, find some brandy for Mrs. Jerrod."

She lifted dark eyes to him. He felt their impact. Despite her obvious distress, the fear still gripping her, there was a violent femaleness about her that struck out at him like a blow.

"No, thank you," she said huskily. "I'll be all right. But I'd like to get home—to Sangaree."

11

"Your husband, he'll need more help . . . ?"

"Park?" She seemed to have forgotten her fear and the warning she had cried out. "He'll be all right. He always has been."

It was a strange statement, but Craig wasted no time with it at the moment. He turned to the bartender. "You might as well have those three guns. Nobody here's going to need them."

"Obliged," the bartender said. His eyes slid to the body on the floor. "What you going to do with Pete Luvain, mister?"

Mrs. Jerrod seemed to have fully recovered. She said, "We can take him to the undertaker in Sangaree."

"That'll do for tonight," Craig agreed. "And tomorrow I'll deliver him to his brother."

II

ANITA JERROD was a strange woman, Craig thought. She seemed to have forgotten entirely the incident that only a short while before had frozen her with fear. And now she chatted almost gaily as though the grisly burden tied to the saddle of the big gray horse tied to Craig's paint didn't even exist.

She rode sidesaddle and so whenever she pointed out something to Craig she had to turn in a way that put the gray and the body of Pete Luvain in her vision. But her only comment was, "Pete was very handsome, but not as handsome as his brother."

And she added, almost casually, "Nor nearly as clever."

"Am I to take that as a warning, Mrs. Jerrod?"

She smiled at Craig; her mouth was full and ripe and her teeth shone whitely in the growing dusk. "I think I would, Mr. . . . ?"

"Craig, Ben Craig."

"Yes, Mr. Craig, I would be very careful of Cloyd Luvain." For the first time since the beginning of their ride, her voice had some body, gave some meaning to her words. "He's not only clever; he's mean. And he loved Pete like—

12

almost like a son. You can't just walk up and shoot him down the way you did Pete."

"I don't expect to," Craig said. "But I'm in no hurry. I can wait until my chance comes."

She was looking straight ahead, toward the growing pinpricks of light that marked the the night's awakening of the town. "You may not get a chance, Mr. Craig. Cloyd might not want to wait to give it to you. If Park doesn't catch those two men, they'll ride straight to Cloyd and tell him what happened. Then he'll come looking for you."

"But not alone," Craig observed. "In all the years I trailed the Luvains, I never heard of them risking themselves. Today, Pete wouldn't even fight your husband without a pair of guns to back him up."

"Why should a man take a risk when he doesn't have to?" she demanded. "You're quite right. Cloyd won't come after you alone. He'll have his army—he controls a dozen men, Mr. Craig, as you'll learn soon enough."

"You seem to know the Luvains quite well," Craig commented.

"They worked for Park from the time they came here until this summer," she answered. Her hand went out, encompassing the land stretching duskily around them. "This is Park's PJ ranch. We don't live on it, of course; his town interests take up more of his time and so we live there. We have a very lovely house. I'm sorry you won't have time to see it."

Craig wondered if she was a little mad, the way her mind seemed to dart from subject to subject. "I may be in Sangaree for some time, waiting for Cloyd, Mrs. Jerrod."

"Oh no. He'll kill you tonight."

The darkness continued to grow as they rode now in silence. But there was still light enough for Craig to see the ricks of hay stacked against the oncoming winter. They looked pitifully small to him.

He said, "How many cattle does the PJ spread run?"

"Around a hundred head," she answered. She laughed, for no reason that Craig could guess. "You're thinking of the haystacks? Our land is very dry, very poor. Park can't grow enough hay and he always has to buy from the big valley

13

ranchers north of town. They have very good land and always more hay than they can use. I think Park envies them their ranches, even if he does own the town and is much richer than they are."

Park Jerrod didn't particularly interest Craig; his one concern here was with Cloyd Luvain. But waiting for the time to kill Luvain might mean spending time in Sangaree—despite what Mrs. Jerrod believed—and Craig had long ago learned that the more he knew about his surroundings, the more able he was to make use of them. He said now, "What do you mean, your husband 'owns' Sangaree?"

"Exactly that. He built it, Mr. Craig. When he came here ten years ago it was nothing but a general store on the flat above the river. Park bought the land, built the stores and the homes, and he brought people in to run the stores and live in the homes. They own their businesses, of course, but Park still owns the land underneath. Sangaree is here only because of him. Just as the ranches in the hills above the valley are here because of him. The three ranchers in the valley were using the hills for extra grazing. Park bought it and then brought ranchers in. He sold them the land very reasonably and helped them stock it."

"He must hold a mortgage on every piece of property in this country," Craig murmured.

"His bank does, except for our home and the hotel and the ranch. Those we own, of course. They're in my name." She added it almost defensively and then said, "Park is very generous."

Something in her voice made Craig uneasy. He said quickly, "It's not my affair, Mrs. Jerrod, but why was Pete Luvain trying to whip your husband this afternoon?"

"Because Park fired him and Cloyd earlier this summer. He found them stealing his cattle and selling them to the so-called miners in the hills north of the valley. You see, it's very profitable to take cattle from here and run them across the border into Canada."

"So when they were fired, Pete and Cloyd joined the miners, is that it?"

"Yes, only very quickly Cloyd became their leader—or so everyone claims. And he has one of those brooding dis-

14

positions—like so many bayou people have. He must have thought and thought about Park's turning him away from the ranch and about the way Park ran him out of town last week—and finally he had Pete go and get revenge on Park. That's what I believe."

She didn't sound particularly incensed at Cloyd Luvain. She added, "Of course, Park had a right to run Cloyd out of town. He and his men came in and started a terrible fight. They have almost everyone in Sangaree terrified. And Park is the local judge."

"Isn't there any law in Sangaree?"

"Only old Marshal Fitchen. And Cloyd and his men tied him up when he tried to stop them. Then Park came and made them clear out. Cloyd was very angry. He and some of his men came back two days later and tore to pieces the saloon where Park had found them. It's just a shell now."

Craig looked at Sangaree ahead of them. This road led directly across a bridge over the river and became the main street. Lights splashed from a number of buildings lining the street and also dotted the hillslope that started abruptly just to the east. A team and wagon moved up the street, and a few horses stood patiently at hitching rails. As far as Craig could see, it was a quiet enough place on the surface.

As if catching his thoughts, Anita Jerrod said, "Sangaree has always been peaceful. A nice place to live. It still is except when Cloyd goes on one of his drunken tears."

Craig doubted if Cloyd Luvain had to be drunk to go on a tear. From what he had learned following the Luvains, they caused trouble only when it profited them.

"It may be peaceful again soon," he said.

"You're very confident, Mr. Craig."

"A man has to develop something in himself over five years," Craig said. "I developed confidence. Until now I never caught up with the Luvains, but I never lost their trail either. I've always had the feeling that I knew where to look— and mostly I've been right."

"So you developed a belief in yourself, your star?"

"You might call it that."

"And hatred too?"

15

"No," Craig said. "You can't hate somebody you don't know. What I hate is the thing the Luvains stand for—the animal viciousness that too many of these famous gunslingers have in them instead of humanity. They're mostly stupid, misfits. They—and the greedy ones who want to own everything and give nothing—they're the ones who keep the West from developing the way it should."

They were crossing the plank bridge over the river and her words were almost lost in the clatter of hooves on the wood. "That was quite a speech, Mr. Craig."

"My apologies for forgetting myself." Craig said briefly. He reined in at the far end of the bridge. A livery stable was directly on their right, a lantern above the wide doors lighting a sign that read, J. TEAZEL, PROP. HORSES BOARDED. RIGS FOR RENT.

Craig said, "My horse is very tired. I think I'll put him here for the night. He needs a good feed of oats and a rubbing down."

"And Pete Luvain, what about him?"

"I'd be obliged if you'd tell me where I can find the undertaker. As soon as I report to the law, I'll take the body there."

In the dim light from the lantern over the livery and from a saloon across the street and up beyond a large hay and feed store, Craig saw the oddness of her expression.

"You're quite serious, aren't you, Mr. Craig? You don't believe that Cloyd will come here tonight and kill you."

"He may try," Craig said.

She made a shrugging motion. "The undertaker is three houses east of the bank. You can see it up the street, on the corner across from the Sangaree House. The city offices with the marshal's office and the jail are in that log building beyond the bank. You can see its lights."

She reined her blaze-faced sorrel more sharply to her right. "And now if you'll excuse me, Mr. Craig, I'll go home. I'm very tired."

Before he could answer, she had gone, disappearing into darkness beside the livery barn. He heard the clatter of hooves on hard ground and then those faded.

A strange woman, he mused. A woman who was almost

violently feminine without appearing conscious of being so. At the same time, she aroused no interest in him—as a woman. He wondered why a man as obviously competent as Park Jerrod had chosen her to take as a wife. From her speech she was obviously Southern, obviously cultured. And, he added to himself, obviously out of place here.

The paint grew restless and Craig brought himself back to his surroundings. He could feel his own weariness from the long grueling ride, and he was suddenly aware of a deep hunger for food and for rest. He had two distasteful chores to do before he could get either one and the sooner he got them out of the way the better.

He rode to the closed doors of the livery and called out. After a long moment, they came creaking open. A bulky man in bib overalls and a peaked cap peered out. "I was about to go home to supper. If you got business, ride in. If you come to jaw, ride on."

Craig rode in, the gray trailing on the end of its lead reins. "I want food and water and a rubdown for my horse," he said. "And a good stall for the night."

The man spat tobacco juice from under a drooping moustache. "I'll give him water and oats. The night man'll see to the rubdown when he comes on."

He moved toward a lighted cubbyhole in the near corner and came back with a lighted lantern. "Which horse, the paint here or . . . ?" He broke off as his light fell on the body draped belly-down over the gray's saddle. "Almighty, who's that!"

"Pete Luvain," Craig said. He readied himself to step out of the saddle.

"So help me, sure as I'm Joe Teazel, it is, right enough! And he looks plumb dead!"

"Dead," Craig agreed. "I'm taking him to the undertaker."

Teazel held the light closer to the gray. "He's been shot. Who done it?" His voice was high now, jerky.

Craig had expected this sooner or later. He said quietly, "I did."

The liveryman's voice rose and then broke, like a half-grown boy's. "You killed him and then you brought him here—to Sangaree? Are you crazy, mister? You get him

17

outa here. And yourself too—and your horse. All of you, get."

"Ease up," Craig said. "What's the matter with you? The man is dead. He can't cause you any trouble."

"No, but Cloyd can—and he will if he finds I gave any help to the fool who shot his brother." The liveryman turned and hurried away, his lantern bobbing. He came back almost at once, and now a carbine was cradled under one arm, the muzzle aimed at Craig.

"I said for you to get and I meant it! Now!" Without setting down the lantern, he levered the carbine, pushing a shell into the chamber.

"Get!" he screamed.

III

CRAIG SAT the paint outside the livery barn and fought to curb the anger surging inside him. His eyes took in the sagging, dark shell of a small building leaning drunkenly against the north side of the livery. A barely readable sign hanging askew over what had once been the door read, RILEY'S SALOON.

This was the place Mrs. Jerrod had told him about, Craig recalled, the place that Cloyd Luvain and his crew had torn apart only a few days ago—and left like this. His anger drained away more easily now as he began to understand some of Joe Teazel's fear of Cloyd Luvain. Even so, Craig wondered, what kind of people did Sangaree have to let a handful of hardcases frighten them so?

He started up the street, patting the paint and murmuring reassurances. The gray came along docilely, used now to the burden sagging across its saddle. The street was quiet and empty except for a few horses tied to hitching rails here and there. With the judging eye of a man who had seen too many jerry-built, sag-roofed Western towns, Craig had noticed with approval the solid look of most of the buildings, and the air of prosperity about them.

On his right, beyond a vacant lot just north of the deserted saloon, was another saloon, a saddlery, another lot,

-18

and then the long sprawling mercantile that reached full to the corner of the cross street. On his left, the buildings were smaller, more tightly pressed together. North of the darkened bulk of the hay and feed was a small saloon building, a barber shop and bath house, a bakery, and a building that seemed half devoted to women's fancy clothes and half to a small restaurant. Beyond it came quickly an assayer's office, a printing plant, and on the corner a larger structure whose ornately painted sign proclaimed it the Sangaree Land and Investment Counselor Building.

Many of the buildings were dark, but soft yellow light splayed from the windows of the saloons and the restaurant to show the well maintained board sidewalk. A number of the buildings had true second stories, not just false fronts—rooms designed for living in.

Park Jerrod's town was a prosperous one, Craig admitted. He reached the lone cross street and glanced both ways along it. Like the main street, there was no sign of life at this, the dinner hour. To the west, he could see the first light of the rising moon on the river as it made its turn northward and started up the broadening valley. The dark bulk of a big building and the dull glow of a slab burner marked the sawmill there on the river bank. Eastward, the street sloped up into the rising hills. Here rows of lights indicated a number of homes, with the spacing between the lights lessening as the steepness of the street increased. The lights farthest up, Craig guessed, would belong to the biggest and fanciest house—Park Jerrod's.

Across the side street from the Mercantile was a solid, two-story brick building that housed the Sangaree Bank. Craig searched on beyond the bank until he located the log building that Mrs. Jerrod had described as the city offices and jail building. A light shone from the farthest window, and Craig rode up until he was opposite it. Leaving the paint, he crossed the board sidewalk to a door with MARSHAL painted on its upper panel. He tried the latch and found it locked. His knocking brought no response. Out to dinner most likely, he thought.

Mounting the paint and leading the gray, Craig returned to the cross street and started eastward for the undertaker's

19

establishment. He found it quickly, the third house past the alley that ran along the rear of the bank and the log jail north of it. A hearse made to be drawn by a four horse team sat alongside the house and a bulky shed behind indicated where the undertaker did most of his work.

Craig had barely left the saddle when the house door opened and a round little man with a chubby face hard put to hold a sad expression came down toward him. His eyes traveled past Craig to the gray. "My condolences, sir. . . ."

Craig remembered the reaction of the liveryman and he said quickly, "This is Pete Luvain's body. I shot him and I want him left here until tomorrow when I'll take him to his brother."

The chubby man took a backward step, his loose mouth flapping in fear. "Not here! No, sir! Not for all the gold in your saddlebags!"

"You think Cloyd Luvain would like to hear you made me leave Pete's body lying across a saddle all night?" Craig asked softly.

The undertaker sagged. "Leave him," he agreed dully. "But take him away first thing in the morning."

Craig was too tired to do more than nod as he mounted the paint and rode off, glad to be rid of the gray and its burden. He went to the marshal's office again and found it still locked. He looked across the street and down toward the corner at the fancy Sangaree House. He was tempted to go there, get a room, have his supper, and sleep away the weariness of the day. But Park Jerrod's invitation held him in check. He had no desire to be beholden to any man, especially to one who "owned" an entire town.

He recalled the little restaurant down the street and decided to go there for his meal. Perhaps the owner could tell him of some other place to stay the night. Reining the weary paint around, he rode across the side street and on to the restaurant. As he started in, he smelled fresh-baked pie mingled with the odor of steaming stew and hot coffee.

Two men were at the near end of the six stool counter. As Craig took off his hat and slipped onto a stool, they pushed aside half empty coffee cups and walked out. Craig laid his hat where one of them had been sitting.

A girl came up to him. A woman, more properly, Craig thought. She was young but mature, with an oval shaped face made for easy smiling, her mouth full and mobile, her cheekbones high. Wide eyes as gray and smoky as Craig's own followed the two men out and then turned to him questioningly.

"I see that J. Teazel has been around," Craig said dryly. "What did he do, draw my picture?"

From the doorway to the kitchen a sharp voice said, "You're the only stranger in town. So you must be the one Joe Teazel is fussing about."

Craig turned on the stool. The woman who stood in the doorway was an older replica of the girl behind the counter, but with dark hair instead of wheat blonde and with an old maid's gauntness.

Craig said, "I'll save you the trouble—do you want me to go somewhere else to eat?"

The sharp eyes raked him. "Was it a fair fight with Pete Luvain?"

The girl said, "Clara!"

Craig nodded. "She has the right to know." He added thinly, "When I knew who it was, I deliberately shot him. But it was a fair enough fight. I let him clear leather before I drew."

"Then I'll get you your stew—that's all we have tonight, except for pie and coffee. Marnie, set a place for Mr.—"

"Craig. Ben Craig. And I'm obliged."

Clara disappeared into the kitchen. Marnie brought silverware and a mug of coffee. She set them down on the counter. "Why did you want to save us trouble?" Her voice was rich and deep in contrast to Clara's sharp tones.

"According to Joe Teazel, I'm poison in Sangaree."

"He's afraid Cloyd Luvain will come and attack everyone who helped you in any way."

"Maybe he can't be blamed," Craig said. "Mrs. Jerrod told me some of the things that Cloyd has done to this town." He frowned. "But what's the matter with these people? Why don't they stand and fight?"

Clara came with a bowl of stew. "I've asked myself that question," she said. She held the stew above the counter. "And I just got through asking myself if you killed Pete Luvain because you're a bounty hunter."

"No," Craig said. "I'm keeping a promise I made to a friend five years ago. The Luvain brothers took his hospitality when they were lost in the desert. They paid him by stealing his food and water and shooting him and his horse. They left him to die. I found him and he lived long enough to describe the pair to me. I've been on their trail ever since." It was not a story he enjoyed telling. He was not concerned about getting sympathy or understanding. But if these women were willing to risk Cloyd Luvain's anger, he felt he owed them an explanation.

"That sounds like the Luvains," Clara remarked and set down the stew. Her curiosity was obviously not yet satisfied. "You said something about talking to Mrs. Jerrod?"

Craig grinned thinly around a mouthful of hot meat and potatoes. He chewed and swallowed before saying, "I ran into Luvain in that saloon on the pass. He and two bully boys had Mr. and Mrs. Jerrod pinned down with guns and Luvain was getting ready to whip Jerrod with his fists. The bully boys got away and Jerrod went after them. I escorted Mrs. Jerrod here to town. She told me some of the things that have happened here lately."

He had his stew finished and was filling his pipe to smoke with a second mug of coffee when the door opened and a lanky, stoop-shouldered old man stomped into the small room. He had a star pinned to his vest and a worn gun butt sticking up from his holster. He stared at Craig from pale, tired eyes.

"You the one who killed Pete Luvain?"

"That's right, marshal. And relax. After I kill his brother, I'm leaving your country."

"Don't smart mouth me, mister. Are you a bounty hunter or the law from someplace else?" The voice was as tired as the eyes.

"The name is Ben Craig and I'm just a man doing a job," Craig said.

Clara came from the kitchen. "What business is it of

yours, Frank Fitchen?" she demanded. "Pete Luvain wasn't killed in town—and you aren't the law outside it. You aren't even much law inside."

The old man flushed. "You tend to your cooking, Clara Clayton, and let me handle my job. I don't care where Luvain was killed. The man who did it is here—and that means trouble until he gets out. Or do you want Cloyd and his hardcases to break up your place again?"

Clara reached behind the door and brought out a carbine. "This time I'll show him this before I tell him to get out," she said. "And I'll use it if I have to."

"I'm the law here. You let me handle things!"

"You!" she said scornfully. "You're like the rest of the townspeople. When Cloyd Luvain and his men broke up my tables, it wasn't you that came to help—nor anybody else but Park Jerrod. He was the only man in town with the gumption to stand up to Luvain. And he drove him off alone."

"This has always been a peaceful town," Fitchen said defensively. "It's my job to see it stays that way." He turned back to Craig. "You have got one half hour to finish your meal and get on your horse and ride."

Craig studied the marshal. Old and tired, he thought sadly. He had seen a lot of them in five years—good lawmen gone to seed and looking for soft dirt to burrow into where they could lie peaceful and quiet and rot away their last days. They wanted nothing to disturb their little piece of garden.

But he felt a greater pity for a town that had to depend on a man like this. He said, "Marshal, my horse has seventy hot, long miles under him since sunup. I'm not riding him any farther tonight."

"Thirty minutes!" The old man started for the door. "Or I'll have you run out."

"You can find enough men to run me away but not enough to stand up against Cloyd Luvain, is that it?"

The door slammed in answer to him. Marnie Clayton said softly, "Why did you rowel him that way?"

"I never ran from a fight," Craig said. "I don't intend to

23

start now. Besides, why should I hunt Luvain down when it seems as if all I have to do is wait—and let him come here to me?"

IV

PARK JERROD ran his black for a good two miles through a maze of twisting canyons before he came within hailing distance of Jenks and Shorty. Dusk was beginning to clamp down and Jerrod was barely able to separate horses and men from canyon wall shadows.

"Hold up, you fools!" he cried. "I have a message for Cloyd!"

The blotches of shadow remained motionless and silent. Jerrod swore softly and slipped his carbine from its boot. He rode forward cautiously. But the shadows stayed as they were, and finally he realized that he was easing up on a shoulder of rock, not two men.

He cursed loudly this time. In answer, a horse and rider appeared, swinging around the shoulder of rock in a wide turn so as to come up on Jerrod at an angle. Jerrod started to rein about and stopped as a whiplash voice cut through the quickening dark at him.

"Hold it right there. Slide that rifle back in its boot."

Jerrod recognized Cloyd Luvain's rumbling voice. "What the devil's the matter with you?" he demanded. "Since when do you throw down on me?"

"The boys told me what happened to Pete back at the saloon." The voice was flat, frighteningly without emotion.

Jerrod slid the carbine back into its boot and turned, riding close enough to Cloyd Luvain to be able to see him more clearly. Luvain was massive in the saddle, a larger version of his brother, but so much like him in the face that they could have been twins. Cloyd Luvain's chiseled features were cast hard and ugly as he stared at Jerrod.

"Don't be a fool," Jerrod snapped. "I never saw that man before this afternoon. He came out of nowhere, asked Pete his name and—when he found out—jockeyed Pete into drawing and then shot him."

"And you just stood there!"

"The devil—so did Jenks and Shorty. I didn't even know what was happening until it was over."

Cloyd Luvain was implacable. "But you jumped Jenks quick enough!"

"And I'll do it again. What right does scum like that have to hold a gun on Park Jerrod?"

"Because I told him to."

Jerrod leaned forward, both hands gripping the saddle horn. "And what right do you have? You're alive because I let you be—remember that. You're what you are because I allowed it. And you're going to be a big man because of me. Remember that, by God!"

"What you done for me—you done for yourself alone," Cloyd said heavily. "And as for the rest of it, I can be as big as I want when I want. I've got the men now, Jerrod. You haven't. I've got the power to take over the Sangaree. You can't do it without me!"

He shifted in the saddle. "I told you last week the boys was restless for the money you owe. You got warned enough what would happen if you didn't pay up. I sent Pete to knock a little sense into you—and he gets himself killed."

Anger seemed to explode inside him, as if saying the words had suddenly released his emotions. He cried, "I want the man who shot Pete—and I want him quick. My God, Pete...."

Jerrod could feel no pity for Luvain, even seeing the depth of his grief, even knowing it was probably the one honest feeling Cloyd had had since his childhood.

He said quietly, "I don't even know his name. But I saved him for you. I told him to put up at the Sangaree House at my expense. I figured you might want a crack at him."

"Tonight," Cloyd Luvain said. "Right now is when I want to get him, the dirty bounty hunter—or whatever he is."

"Stop and think," Jerrod snapped. "Pete's dead. You can't bring him back by getting yourself killed. And that's what'll happen if you go charging the stranger like a crazy bull. He's quick—quicker than any man I ever saw. And he's out to kill you just like he killed Pete. Use your head. Hold off a little—and it'll pay us plenty."

Cloyd Luvain swore viciously. Then he fell silent, as if he had drained himself by the violence of his emotional explosion. He sat broodingly on his smoke horse, staring empty-eyed at Jerrod. Finally, he said, "Keep talking."

"If you ride into town and try to kill the stranger now, you'll have to bring your crew. You can't do it alone. And if you bring them and raise a ruckus the way you did the last time, the town won't stand for it. You can push people around just so much. Sooner or later they're going to fight back."

"Rabbits, the lot of them," Cloyd Luvain said contemptuously.

"Even a rabbit will fight if it's protecting its young or its hole," Jerrod said quietly. "I told you to stop and think—do it. You spent the summer working hard to take stock from the valley ranchers and make it look as if the hill men did it. You did a good job—Truesdale and Kearney and Finch are ready to ride on the hill ranchers and burn them out. One big move and we can make them do it! And as I told you, when we do, the whole valley floor will be ours—yours and mine. Once you get your piece of that, you'll be ready to get your share of the town. And that's big money."

"I know the plans," Cloyd said impatiently. "What have they got to do with the stranger that killed my brother?"

"I can figure a way to use him, to make it look like his coming here is what caused all the trouble. That'll take the blame off you, make you look good in the eyes of the town. That's important when you get ready to take over your half of it."

"You ain't making sense," Cloyd complained.

Jerrod was a man whose mind worked quickly. He had long ago decided that if he acted on his first impulses he was more likely to be successful. He said now, talking as his mind formed the ideas, "We'll make a hero out of the stranger. That's easy enough for me to do. Then we'll set it up so Marshal Fitchen gets himself killed or resigns. Someway I'll fix it so the stranger gets maneuvered into becoming the local law, not just in town but in the valley as well." He

26

paused briefly and then went on, speaking more rapidly.

"All right, what happens when the valley ranchers finally attack the hill men? The stranger will have to ride out and try to stop the trouble. Then . . ."

Cloyd Luvain laughed harshly. "Then me and the boys ride down and stop the fighting. The stranger ends up dead—with my bullet in him. And I'm the peacemaker. I'm the one those town jokers'll think stopped a range war!"

"That's it exactly. And don't forget, you can get a lot more milk out of a cow that trusts you than one that runs for cover every time she gets your smell up her nose."

"What makes you think the stranger'll hold still for all this?"

"He'll stay until he gets his chance to kill you," Jerrod said. "We'll see that he doesn't get the chance—not until we're ready for you to kill him."

"How long do I have to wait to get my chance?"

"Not long. The valley men will have to be pushed into fighting the hill ranchers before the first snow falls. And that isn't far off now."

Cloyd Luvain was silent again. Then he nodded, a motion that Jerrod was barely able to see in the darkness. Cloyd said slowly, "What about Pete—Pete's body?"

"I'll see that Marley makes him a fine coffin and I'll have it brought to you."

"No. I want him buried proper, in the town cemetery. And quick. When me and Pete left home, I promised Ma that if anything happened to Pete, he'd get a proper burying. I'm keeping that promise. And I made a promise to Pete too. He liked moonlight. He told me once he wanted to be buried in the moonlight." He glanced eastward. "It's about full now."

Jerrod hesitated. Then he said, "You can have it any way you want. The moon will be full in two days. I'll fix it so you and the boys can have the funeral night after tomorrow. And you can get a look at the stranger then. By that time, I'll know more about him."

"You see that Marley gives Pete the best coffin he's got—and the best lot in the cemetery too."

"I'll handle it," Jerrod promised.

27

Cloyd started to turn his horse and stopped. "What about the money? The boys spent all they made pushing that last bunch of valley stock across the border. They're getting mighty thirsty."

"I'll have that for you night after tomorrow too. When the funeral's finished, meet me. You know where."

"I know where. And this time you better have the money. Talk don't buy you much anymore."

"I'll have it," Jerrod snapped. He reined the black around and rode away. He had taken more time than he'd planned and now he wanted to get to Sangaree and take care of his business there. But the moon had yet to rise and it was some while before he managed to work his way out of the maze of canyons and onto the wagonroad. Once headed for town, he let the black have its head while he let his mind work on all the problems facing him.

Cloyd's insistence on getting paid for rustling cattle that he sold for big money annoyed Jerrod, but he knew from the man's attitude that he would have to bring hard cash to their next meeting. As he rode, he thought he had found a solution to that problem and he set it aside.

He considered the funeral. He would have to prepare the townspeople for the idea. He didn't want any trouble, not at this stage of things. He was too close to fulfilling his dream of owning the rich valley ranches instead of the miserable scrub land he was riding through now. Making that dream come true had about strapped him. For all the wealth he drew from Sangaree, of late he had paid most of it to Cloyd Luvain and his crew. And in addition he had had to support the hill ranchers, since most of them were still new to the country and had yet to build herds big enough to bring them a profit. But if it cost him every penny he could find—or steal—owning the valley, owning the land that the big three had so often flatly refused to sell, would be worth everything.

Jerrod swore as a new thought struck him. What if Cloyd got drunk before he came to Pete's funeral? Jerrod had seen the big man drunk often enough to know how he would act. Each time, Cloyd had become almost maudlin about Pete, mouthing about how he had vowed to take

28

care of his little brother. At the same time he took on a new viciousness so that if any man so much as looked sideways at Pete, Cloyd was all over him, fighting like a crazed animal. More than once he had had to be stopped from beating to death one of his own crew.

If Cloyd should get drunk and then bring his men to the funeral, Jerrod could imagine what would happen. Cloyd would forget his agreement to wait before killing the stranger. He would not only lose his caution and try to kill the stranger, but he would wreck the town that had harbored the man.

Tomorrow, Jerrod thought, he would ride to Goldbar and warn some of Cloyd's men to keep him sober. They would understand; they were more afraid of Cloyd when he was drunk than when he wasn't.

Satisfied that he had temporarily solved his most pressing problems, Jerrod put spurs to the black and sent it rocketing toward the nearing lights of Sangaree.

When the hoofbeats of Jerrod's horse had faded, Cloyd Luvain rode back around the shoulder of rock where Jenks and Shorty waited, carbines in their hands. "Put them guns away. Jerrod ain't got the belly for killing me." He laughed harshly. "Besides, he needs me too bad,"

"From what he said, it sounds like you need him too," Shorty ventured.

"The devil I do! And when the big fight starts between the valley ranchers and those jokers in the hills, who do you think is going to get my bullet in his brisket? Mr. Park Jerrod—Mr. own-it-all, know-it-all Jerrod, that's who! I'm going to own the valley and the town, and I ain't going to pussyfoot about it the way he wants neither.

"Now let's get riding. I want to do some talking with the boys. And I want a drink, a whole herd of drinks. I got me some thinking to do."

"What about the stranger? You going to wait to kill him like Jerrod told you?" Jenks asked.

"That's what I got to do my thinking about," Cloyd said roughly. He sucked in a deep breath. "He ain't going to get just a quick bullet out of the dark. No, by God, when

29

he dies, he's going to do it slow. He's going to know who gutshot him. And he's going to lie there and wish he never fooled with the Luvain brothers!"

V

CRAIG held a match to his pipe. "Why is everyone so afraid of Luvain?" he asked. "From what Mrs. Jerrod told me, her husband should be the only one to really fear him. But he stands up to Luvain when nobody else will."

"Jerrod built this town," Clara said. "Maybe that's why he's willing to fight for it. And he works hard to raise beef on that scrub land of his. Maybe that's why he couldn't stand to have the Luvains steal from him."

"Did they take only his stock?" Craig asked. "What about those rich looking ranches to the north? And the ranches in the hills?"

"Oh, the valley men lost plenty of stock," Clara said. "But the hill men haven't got anything worth taking yet. They haven't been here long enough to build up decent herds."

Craig persisted in his questioning, wanting to know more about this country that harbored Cloyd Luvain. "Why haven't the big ranchers gone after Luvain? Are they afraid too?"

Marnie answered. "They aren't very friendly men, Mr. Craig. They were here first and they had the run of the whole valley and the hills until Mr. Jerrod found that a lot of the land was railroad owned—given the railroads by the government even though they've never come close to here. Then he bought up the land and brought in the hill ranchers. The valley men tried to run them off at first but Mr. Jerrod had legal titles to the land and he made them back off. Ever since, they've been convinced that the hill ranchers are the ones taking their cattle—out of spite and to keep themselves alive."

Feuds, Craig thought wearily. If it wasn't land or water or timber it was something else that one man owned and another man wanted—even if that other man already had more than his share.

He glanced toward the window but it was steamed up and he could see nothing through it. Paying for his food, he slid off the stool and took up his hat. "Thank you for your hospitality," he said.

"And just where are you going?" Clara asked in her blunt way.

"To find a place for my horse—and myself."

"There's a stable behind the Sangaree House," she said. "And that's the only place in town with any rooms. The boardinghouse is full."

Then it would have to be the Sangaree House, he thought. But he'd make sure he paid his own way rather than let Jerrod do it for him. With a brief good night, he stepped outside and started for the paint. He stopped in surprise. A sizable crowd was gathered on the sidewalk.

A tubby little man with a deep, rusty voice cried, "There he comes. There's the stranger who shot Pete Luvain!"

Face set, Craig swung his heavy shoulders, pushing his way to his horse. He climbed into the saddle. "Fall back," he ordered. "I want to ride away from here."

"Ride where?" the rusty-voiced man called. "There ain't a man in town with a spare bed that'll let you borrow it—not in Sangaree!"

A small, slim man at the edge of the crowd called, "If you have trouble here, sir, accept my hospitality. I'll be pleased to feed you and your horse all winter for what you've done."

"And why not?" a deep, angry voice demanded. It came from a big man, wide and solid in expensive ranch clothing. "You don't have to be afraid of Luvain, Thackaberry. Why would he bother a man who steals my beef for him to sell across the border?"

The small man turned with no sign of fear. He stared steadily at the rancher bulking over him. "Mr. Kearney," he said in his cultured voice, "I have everything I need. I don't find it necessary to steal from you. I've paid cash money or worked to raise every head of stock on my place. Now

31

if you think you have a prosecutable case against me or Dwyer or Cardon, then I suggest you take us to court. If you don't, let me remind you that there are laws to protect a man from slander!"

"I've heard that kind of lawyer talk before," Kearney rumbled. "But it doesn't mean a thing to me—not when I saw with my own eyes my beef and Finch's and Truesdale's mixed with those scrubs belonging to you hill scum—and the whole herd drifting easy as you please north toward the border." He thrust his face forward. "And don't tell me about the law! In the valley, I'm my own law. And the next time any valley beef disappears, you'll find out what that means!"

He swung away, stomping up the sidewalk toward the Sangaree House. The rusty-voiced man let out a whoop. "Range war! That's what Kearney just declared, a range war!"

"If this stranger doesn't get out of town, it won't be a range war you'll have to worry about, Briggs," a new voice said. "It'll be Cloyd Luvain and his crew doing what they did to Riley's saloon."

Craig, from his vantage point on the paint, spotted the speaker, a nervous looking man in a business suit. He was flanked on one side by Joe Teazel and on the other by a stocky, moustached man who had the air of a barkeep. The burned-out Riley? Craig wondered.

"Just what is your stake in Sangaree?" Craig called to the man.

"My name is Wallace," he answered. "I run the sawmill here. I've worked hard to make it what it is. I don't intend to see it burned down because of a fight that isn't my affair."

"Pride in your city and defending yourself against a bully like Luvain should be your affair," Craig snapped. He let his eyes sweep over the crowd. "But from what I heard, there's only one man willing to stand up and fight for what he has!"

"He means Mr. Jerrod," Briggs called out rustily. "But I'll fight, mister. I would if I had the price of a gun!"

No one laughed. Wallace said, "You can talk. Maybe you're like Luvain and know how to stand up to his kind.

But what chance have we got against a dozen professional gunslicks?"

Before Craig could answer, a horse came up the street, pushed hard by its rider. Craig recognized Jerrod and his black gelding.

Jerrod pulled up at the edge of the crowd. "What's going on here?" he demanded. His voice was sharp with weariness.

"The marshal and these folks here seem to want this stranger out of town before Cloyd Luvain comes and spanks 'em all," Briggs called.

Jerrod's dark gaze raked over the crowd. Craig saw men turn away and then some began to drift off as Jerrod's voice cut at them. "You sniveling cowards! This man saved my life today. He's here at my invitation. Now move aside and let him get his horse through. Go home and hide in your beds!"

A path opened for Craig and he rode the paint into the street. Jerrod ran the black alongside. "I expected you to be in the hotel by this time."

"I'm not sure they'd have taken me in," Craig said dryly. He glanced back. The only men who had not started away were Briggs and the hill rancher, Thackaberry. He said, "That Briggs is quite a joker."

"He tries to put gumption in those people," Jerrod said. "But shaped the way he is, he only gets ignored—or laughed at. And then he won't work at a regular job, just helps around here and there. He claims he's a philosopher."

He waved Briggs aside. "I lost those two men in the hills. But I don't think Luvain will come here after you—not right away, unless he rides in to get his brother's body."

"And if he does come and wants to fight—how many men can you count on to stand against him?"

"Myself, the old man who runs the mercantile, Briggs, the hill ranchers if they're in town, and a man or two from the saloons—if they're liquored enough to have their courage up."

"But not the marshal?"

"Not the marshal," Jerrod agreed. They reached the cross street and he reined west, alongside the hotel. "We'll

33

put our horses in the stable," he said. "Then I'd be obliged if you'd have supper with me."

"I ate," Craig said. Then, to soften his abruptness, he added, "But I'll take coffee. You can ask me your questions then."

Jerrod's smile was tight. "I'll do just that."

A gnome of a man took the horses and scowled at Craig as he was given instructions on feeding and rubbing down the paint. Jerrod led the way into the lobby through a rear door and down a long hallway. Craig glanced around, noticing the ornateness of the place. The rich paneled woods and the fancy chandelier had obviously been brought in at great expense. To the right doors opened onto a softly lighted saloon-bar, and on the left he glimpsed a dining room with white cloths on the tables. Only a few people were dining.

"The clerk will register you," Jerrod said. "We'll meet in the dining room." He strode away, leaving Craig with saddlebags slung over his shoulder.

Craig found his room as comfortable and well furnished as the lobby had led him to expect. He washed, changed his shirt, and returned to the lobby and went into the dining room. Jerrod was seated at a side table and already well into his meal.

"I ordered you brandy to go with your coffee."

"My pleasure," Craig said. He sat down and reached for his pipe. "Mrs. Jerrod told me how you came and built everything that's here," he said. "I wondered why a man would come this far from nowhere to start an empire?"

Jerrod chuckled. "That's blunt enough. I came here from Alder Gulch, my saddlebags stuffed with gold. I found cheap land in a beautiful setting and only four families in the whole place—three ranchers and old Mason, who runs the mercantile. I wanted what I saw. I was raised in an Eastern city, after my father lost his land to sharpers. I swore when I was a boy to own land myself, more than he ever had. When I saw the Sangaree, I knew it was my place. I stayed."

Craig's coffee and brandy came. Jerrod waited until he had warmed himself with a sip of the liquor and then asked,

34

"You told Pete Luvain you'd been hunting him for five years because he'd killed a friend of yours. Is that the only reason?"

"It's reason enough," Craig said quietly. He lit his pipe. "The man the Luvains killed was my friend. I was a lieutenant in the Cavalry in Arizona. Chalco was our chief scout. I heard rumors of an Indian gathering to the west of Tuscon and I ordered him to find out what he could. He didn't want to go—he'd had one of those premonitions soldiers get—but because we were friends, he did as I I asked. The Luvains had been down in Sonora and they stole a gold train, killed the Mexicans, and drove the mules up into Arizona. They got lost on the desert, in the hot country where Chalco was camped. He took them in, gave them food and water, and the next day they shot him, took everything but his horse, put a bullet in that, and rode off. I found him a quarter of a mile from a waterhole, burned to nothing by the sun, his horse dead of thirst. He lived long enough to describe the Luvains for me. He died in my arms. I swore I'd get them."

"And that was five years ago?"

"Five years," Craig agreed. "I resigned my commission and went after them. But they stayed one jump ahead of me—in Texas, in Colorado, in New Mexico Territory, in Wyoming. I learned a lot about them but I never saw either one until today."

"It takes money to spend five years on the trail."

"I worked here and there, driving cattle, as a lawman, in the mines. Finally I heard they were in Montana. I got to Fort Benton and an old-timer told me they were here and had been for some time."

"So you came—and found one. What will you do when you kill the other? If you do."

"Go home," Craig said. "My brother is running the family place out in Oregon. It's land outside the town of Portland. I figure on letting him run the cattle and I'll breed horses." His smile was thin. "And I'll get Cloyd Luvain. If not tomorrow, then the next day or the next. I can wait."

Jerrod lifted his coffee cup and set it down as two men came into the dining room. One was young, solidly built,

35

wearing range clothes that had seen a lot of work. The other was the marshal.

Fitchen reached the table first. He put a hand on his gun butt and glared at Craig. "I told you to ride out of Sangaree, mister!"

"This man is my guest," Jerrod said. "Even if I don't know what to call him." He nodded as Craig gave his name.

The marshal kept his eyes on Craig. "I'm the law here, Mr. Jerrod. And this stranger is nothing but trouble—just as we thought." He motioned to the young man. "Tell him, Dwyer."

Dwyer said quickly, "I was up near Goldbar earlier hunting some strays and I stopped in the saloon for a drink before starting home. It was dark and getting cold. While I was there, Cloyd Luvain and two of his men came in. Cloyd was crazy mad and yelling about somebody killing Pete! He started drinking and talking about coming here to get the man who shot Pete.

"I slipped away before Luvain eased up enough to pay any attention to me. I was on the crest trail nearly home when I looked down in the valley and saw 'em riding— Luvain and his whole crew. They're coming here and Luvain's drunk enough to tear Sangaree apart."

Jerrod turned bleak eyes on the marshal. "And your idea is to do what—send Craig into the valley to meet Luvain so he can be killed and then Luvain can ride home happy?" His tone was like a knife of ice.

"He'll be here in half an hour," Fitchen said. "What else is there to do?"

"Fight," Craig answered. "Deputize some men and go to the edge of town and turn Luvain back. I know what he's like. He won't stand up to more men than he has backing him."

"There aren't that many who'll face him," Jerrod said quietly.

"Then do it with those who will!" Craig snapped.

"Go see how many you can get," Jerrod told the marshal. "I'll be along presently." He lifted his cup again.

The old man took a deep, stubborn breath. "I'm the law here, Mr. Jerrod, and that ain't my way of handling it! I want Craig out of town. You might be the judge here but I'm still the law!"

Craig said, "Sorry, marshal, but I've spent five years waiting to kill Luvain. If he's coming here, I'll stay and welcome him. If I have to do it alone, then I will."

Fitchen looked at Jerrod and Jerrod said, "If you're the law, act like it, old man."

Fitchen took another breath. Then with shaking fingers he unpinned his star and slapped it down by Craig. "If he knows so much about handling Luvain, let him have the job. When I took this job, I told you I was my own man. I still am." And turning, he stalked away, his shoulders straight for the first time since Craig had seen him.

"That took a kind of courage I didn't think he had," Craig said.

Jerrod pushed the star forward. "Well?" He added, "Fitchen is right. You talk big about Luvain. Now will you do something about him?"

Craig pushed back his chair and picked up the star. "It looks," he said softly, "that if Sangaree wants to get its peace and quiet back, it's going to have to fight for them—beginning now."

He pinned on the star. "You maneuvered me into this, Jerrod, but I'm like Fitchen. I'm my own man, not yours. As long as I'm the law here, I'll run things my own way."

"And how long will that be?"

"Until I've killed Cloyd Luvain," Craig said. He started for the door.

VI

JERROD caught up with Craig in the lobby, Dwyer at his heels. "Well, *marshal*," Jerrod said with soft mockery, "What's your first move?"

"I'll want all the men willing to stand up to Luvain to meet in front of the hotel as quickly as possible," Craig said. "And as many as we can get should be on horses." He glanced at Dwyer. "You," he added, "what's your position in this?"

37

"I'll help all I can," Dwyer said. "Maybe if I get a chance to stand against Luvain those valley ranchers'll stop thinking us hill men are part of the gang."

"You could shoot Luvain in front of Kearney's eyes and he wouldn't believe you," Jerrod said. "Because he doesn't want to believe. All right, see who you can dredge up out of the saloons."

Craig said heavily, "And you might tell those who want to run and hide to warn their friends to find holes to crawl into." He turned to Jerrod. "I'll need a fresh horse for myself."

Dwyer moved away, out the front door and down the street. Jerrod led Craig to the stable and ordered horses saddled for both of them. "I'll give Dwyer a hand with spreading the news," he said. "You'd be wise to plan your strategy. Even if Luvain is drunk, you won't find him a fool. He's smart and he's clever."

"So I've been told," Craig said. He looked northward, up the alley where they stood waiting for the horses. "How far does the law reach?"

"From the river on the south and west to the crest of the hills above my house on the east and at the end of this alley north," Jerrod said. "Go up the main street and when you've passed the boardinghouse on your left and the stand of timber on your right, you're out of Sangaree."

The horses were brought out and Craig mounted, noticing with satisfaction that both were dark-coated animals without any white markings. With a nod to Jerrod, he started his animal up the alley. Beyond the corner of the Sangaree House was a sprawl of vacant ground, then two small houses, another stretch of weed-grown land, and finally the two-story boardinghouse. All three buildings showed light and Craig called at each to have the lamps put out. He had only to mention Luvain's coming and he got no argument.

Leaving the boardinghouse, he trotted his horse across the street and studied the stand of timber. It was spotty, thick and with heavy undergrowth in some places, thin with barren ground in others. Nodding, he rode back down the main street, noticing that between the timber and the jail there was only bare, empty ground.

When he reached the front of the hotel, he found a knot of half a dozen people waiting. He recognized Thackaberry and Briggs, who somewhere had managed to find an ancient, long-barreled rifle. He guessed that the old man in the buggy with a vintage Sharps across his knees was John Mason. The fourth man, red-faced from a little too much liquor, he hadn't seen before. The last of the six were Clara Clayton and Marnie. They stood quietly on the sidewalk, each holding a carbine.

Craig said, "This is no game for ladies."

Marnie said softly, "Clara and I were raised on a ranch, Mr. Craig. We can use these guns."

Before Craig could answer, Jerrod rode up with a heavy-set, bleary-eyed man beside him. "This is all, I expect. The rest have run for their holes." He pointed to the man beside him. "This is Arty Logan, marshal. He works for Kearney. The other one there is Buck Mulligan, a hand for Finch in the valley. And this gentleman is John Mason. He owns the Mercantile."

He glanced at the two women. "And don't sell the Clayton sisters short, marshal. Clara can put a bullet through the eye of a needle at fifty feet. Marnie isn't quite as good a shot. She'd hit the needle."

Arty Logan and Buck Mulligan laughed the way half-drunk men will, easing the tension a little. Jerrod said to Dwyer, "How many men did Luvain have with him?"

"I'd guess a dozen," Dwyer answered. He frowned as he glanced northward. "He'll be here inside of ten minutes, Mr. Jerrod."

Jerrod nodded. "It's your play now, marshal."

Craig said quickly, "I'll want three lines of defense. Mr. Mason, if you and Briggs here could each take a side of the street—one of you in the jail, the other in those shadows across the way—you can make up the second line." He turned to Clara and Marnie. "I'd be obliged if you ladies would take an upstairs room in the hotel. The northeast corner is best, then you'll have two windows to shoot from."

"That's my apartment," Jerrod said. "And they're welcome."

"We don't appreciate your effort at chivalry," Marnie said.

"It isn't chivalry," Craig snapped. "It's common sense. You haven't got horses under you and you're both said to be fine shots." The snap stayed in his voice, as if he had forgotten he no longer held his Cavalry commission. Thackaberry, can you and Mulligan here take the shadows alongside the boardinghouse up ahead? And Dwyer, I want you and Logan to go into that stand of timber. Take a spot where you can have shelter and still see the road north of the town limits."

He pointed up the moonlit street. "The trees and the boardinghouse both cast good shadows while the road past them is in full moonlight. That's where we stop Luvain so that he's in the light and we aren't."

"And where will you and I be, marshal?" Jerrod wanted to know.

"At the north edge of the timber, just in the shadows," Craig answered. "I'm hoping Luvain will listen if you call out to him to hold up. You *are* the local judge. You've stopped him before."

"And what if my being judge won't make him listen?"

"Then we'll do what we have to," Craig said. He glanced at the others. "Nobody shoots until he hears me tell him to. Not even if Jerrod and I have to use our guns—not until you get the word."

Not waiting to see if the women followed orders and went into the hotel, Craig started his horse up the street, the others following. He saw old John Mason wheel his buggy into shadows across from the jail and watched Briggs go into the building. The tubby little man was strutting some, obviously enjoying his role. Farther along, Thackaberry and Mulligan, a little less drunk now, faded into darkness beside the boardinghouse and Dwyer and Arty Logan slipped into the trees. Craig rode to the spot he had seen earlier and pulled his horse into a thick finger of shadow thrown by the timber at his back. Jerrod joined him.

"This is a good spot," Jerrod said dryly. "You can

shoot Luvain out of the saddle before he even knows you're close."

"No," Craig said flatly. "I'll give him the same chance I gave his brother. But I won't even call him tonight if he listens to reason."

Jerrod had his gun half drawn from his holster. "You wait five years for this chance and then turn away from it?"

"You made the point yourself earlier," Craig said. "By staying here, I brought Luvain down on Sangaree. That's why I took your law job. And as long as I have it, I won't shoot any man except to defend myself or the town. When I'm ready to kill Luvain, then I'll resign. Unless he forces my hand sooner."

Jerrod muffled a soft sigh of relief and let the gun slide back in its holster. "Are you going to let Luvain know who you are?"

"If I have to," Craig answered.

"He'll go berserk," Jerrod warned. "If he's still drunk, God knows what he'll do with his brother's killer so close to him."

"That's the risk I take," Craig said. He reached out and touched Jerrod, cautioning silence. For the first time, he could hear something up ahead on the cold, clear air.

"Move apart," he whispered, "they're coming."

Jerrod eased his horse sideways, some ten feet from Craig's position. Now the sounds were sharper—the steady clop of hooves, the jangle of harness. But there was no sound of voices, no raucous singing or shouting as there usually was when Luvain and his men got drunk and rode to Sangaree. Nor were the riders coming very fast.

It might, Craig thought, be a funeral procession, from the speed the horses were making.

The first rider rode close enough for Craig to take in the heavy body, the neat, tight features, even the strong forward slant of the Spanish rig on his horse—all sharp and clear under the bright moon.

Cloyd Luvain!

It took the full force of Craig's will to keep him from drawing and shooting Luvain out of the saddle. He made himself sit calmly, to keep silent instead of shouting out his challenge. This was no time for fighting. This wasn't his fight alone, not with the safety of a whole town resting on him.

Behind Luvain came a full dozen men riding closely packed and three abreast. When Luvain was within twenty feet of the end of the tongue of shadow, Jerrod lifted his voice.

"That's far enough, Cloyd. You and your crew aren't wanted in Sangaree tonight."

Luvain jerked his horse to a halt and whipped out his .44 in the same motion. He leaned forward, his eyes probing the darkness. "Jerrod? Where the devil are you?"

"Sitting my horse with a carbine aimed at your belly," Jerrod answered coolly.

"One gun against thirteen!" Cloyd Luvain laughed. His voice was only slightly slurred, just enough to tell that some of the whiskey was still working in him.

"Not just one gun," Craig called back. "All right, you men to the west. Move around. Let them hear you. And all of you behind us too."

Luvain's head swiveled to his left as harness jingled from that direction. Then it whipped to the right as Dwyer and Arty Logan did a fine job of trampling dry twigs underfoot. If Craig hadn't known differently, he would have thought a small army stood behind him.

"Who are you?" Luvain demanded. "Ride out and let me have a look. I ain't never heard your voice before."

"You'll hear more of it than you want before we're done," Craig said. "I'm the new marshal here and I'm telling you to turn your horses and ride for home."

Jenks pulled up closer to Luvain's big smoky horse. "That's the stranger talking!" he cried. "That's the one who shot Pete!"

Cloyd Luvain gave a half strangled cry of rage, jerked up his gun and fired blindly into the darkness. The bullet thudded into a tree a good five feet to Craig's left. Coolly, Craig drew his own gun and fired, sending Luvain's hat spinning from his head.

"Next time I'll lower my sights a few inches," he said. He edged his horse sideways.

42

Luvain's gun sprayed lead wildly through the darkness, the sound of his firing only half drowning his shouted curses. Craig called over the deep roar of the .44. "All right, men, start their horses jumping!"

Bullets came snapping from the darkness, striking the moonlit road near the hooves of the tightly packed horses. One animal rose up, neighing in terror and jolting his rider from the saddle. Others on the outside turned into the pack, starting a wild milling of horses and cursing riders.

Luvain rode forward, charging Craig like a man crazed beyond endurance. Craig swung to his right, to the very edge of the shadows. "That's far enough, Luvain!" he snapped.

Luvain reined his horse toward the sound of Craig's voice and sent the big animal thundering ahead. At the same time, he brought his gun up and fired.

VII

CRAIG had sent his horse out of the shadows and into the moonlight, so Luvain's bullet whined harmlessly away in the dark. Now Craig brought up his gun and as Luvain came even with him, fired. Luvain cried out as his own .44 was sent spinning from his hand. He fought his horse to stop but not before he was deep in the fingers of shadow.

Craig reined quickly around and sent his horse alongside Luvain's. He pulled up and put the muzzle of his gun against the side of Luvain's neck. "How many times do you have to be told?" he demanded softly.

"You've got one last chance to sober up and ride home," Jerrod said from Luvain's other side. "Isn't that right, Marshal?"

"Marshal!" Luvain cried. "What right have you got to make Pete's killer the law in Sangaree?"

"Just be thankful he hasn't killed you too," Jerrod said. "From what I heard, Craig has given you more chance than you ever gave Chalco."

"Chalco—Jenks told me what this stranger said about

43

him. Hell, I don't even remember anything except he was a breed."

"That's going to make it a double pleasure for me to kill you when the time comes," Craig said thinly. "Now make up your mind, Luvain. You can ride back out there and start your men fighting us or you can take them on home."

Luvain's voice was low, his drawl heavy as he said, "You gents got it all wrong. We didn't come here to fight tonight. You pushed us into it. We came to bury Pete."

Craig had to admire the man's acting. "I got a right to bury him," Luvain went on. "He was my brother. I got a right to see he gets a proper funeral. And he always wanted to be buried under moonlight. Pete liked moonlight."

"Well, marshal?" Jerrod asked.

"Let them have their funeral," Craig agreed. He said to Luvain, "Ride back there and tell your men to get off their horses and to leave their guns—all of them. You can walk to the cemetery."

"I ain't crazy enough to take my boys into town without guns," Luvain protested. "They'd get shot up for sure!"

"Not tonight, they won't," Craig said. "I'm the law now and I'll see that you're let alone. As long as you don't try any tricks, you're safe enough. If you really came to have a funeral, you don't need guns."

Luvain was silent a moment. Then he said, "All right. But somebody'd better tell Marley to give Pete his best coffin. I'll pay whatever it costs. And have him take shovels and lanterns to the graveyard too." The cold muzzle of Craig's gun moved away from his neck and he carefully backed his horse away from the trees.

His men had finally got their animals under control and they were sitting now, guns in their hands, waiting for orders. Craig sat tensely, waiting to see what Luvain's next move would be. But if he intended to fight, he showed no sign of it. He spoke to his men in a voice too low for Craig to hear.

"It's a trick!" Jenks warned. "He'll kill you sure, Cloyd."

"Not tonight, he won't," Luvain said. "He's had plenty of chances already, ain't he? And he didn't take them. Now do as I say!"

44

Craig and Jerrod watched as the men began to dismount and to remove their guns and belts, hanging them over their saddle horns. Craig said softly, "Dwyer, can you get Thackaberry and Briggs and guard these men? But don't let them see you."

"Glad to, marshal," Dwyer said. There was a touch of awe in his voice. "I never seen anything like the way you handled Luvain!"

"He's been bullying people long enough," Craig said. "It's time he learned a little humility."

"Before he dies," Jerrod said sardonically.

"Before he dies," Craig agreed. He watched the road. Luvain was leading a silent, slow procession down the street. He alone looked only straight ahead. The others kept glancing to one side and then the other, as if expecting to be shot at any instant.

"Luvain took you at your word," Jerrod remarked.

Craig said, "I'd be obliged if you'd make sure that none of the townsmen bother them."

"I'll check the saloons. That's where the trouble'd come from."

"Both of you'd better move quickly," Craig warned. "Briggs and Mason might start shooting first and thinking afterward."

Jerrod and Dwyer rode quickly away, Dwyer swinging out to cross the road and pick up Thackaberry, Jerrod moving down toward the alley mouth that began at the near back corner of the jail building. Craig called Arty Logan over and they rode to where Mulligan stood by the boardinghouse.

"I'd like you two to empty all the guns. Put the bullets in the proper saddlebags," he instructed. "Then string their horses together and stand guard until the funeral is over."

"Sure," Logan said. He sounded sober now.

"I wish our bosses could have seen them hill men tonight," Mulligan said. "Maybe they'd stop thinking they're part of Luvain's gang."

"Not Kearney," Arty Logan answered. "He's even more bullheaded than Finch."

Craig left them arguing about it and rode by the alley

to the Sangaree House. He hurried upstairs to find Clara and Marnie in Jerrod's suite, each standing at an open window, their guns ready.

"They aren't armed," Craig said. "Luvain is going to bury Pete tonight."

"I figured that out," Clara said acidly, "or I'd have used some powder before now." She turned to Craig. "You're taking a big risk. There are men in this town who'd be only too glad to shoot Luvain now that it's safe to do so."

Craig explained what he'd done to protect the procession. "I just hope Dwyer and Thackaberry don't let themselves be seen," he added.

Marnie looked at him curiously. "Why is that important?"

"I don't see why I should let Luvain know they had a hand in this," Craig answered. "He might go after them for it. Besides, no matter what he is, Luvain has a right to his private grief tonight."

"You're an odd one," Clara observed. "You spend five years tracking down a man to kill him and then you show him compassion." She sniffed. "Well, that doesn't make me any money. Come along, Marnie. When the funeral is over, there'll still be a lot of wide-awake people around. They'll be wanting pie and coffee."

She stopped in the doorway. "That includes you, marshal."

Craig waited until they were gone. Then he stood at the window and watched the slowly moving procession turn up the cross street toward the undertaker's. When the last man had rounded the corner of the bank building, he went back outside. It was in his mind to check the saloons, to make sure that no one was building up too much courage with whiskey and so thinking about attacking Luvain and his men.

The town was extraordinarily quiet, even considering the events of this night. Craig found only one saloon open, and that empty but for the bartender dozing on a stool. He walked away, frowning, more concerned than if he had found men drinking and arguing, working themselves up at the thought of Luvain here and virtually helpless. Craig had known many cattle towns—too many, he sometimes thought wearily—and always when a sharp change came

46

about or when a crisis passes, then men would group together and in one way or another give relief to their feelings. He guessed that Jerrod had ordered everyone home.

He walked on, going south toward the river. The small saloon across the street from the dark pile that remained of Riley's place was dark. The night light at Teazel's livery had been extinguished. There was only the moonlight, shadowed by the bulk of the hay and feed store here. And there was silence. Through it Craig could hear the murmur of the river running under the bridge but nothing else, not even the stirring of the horses in the livery barn.

His frown deepened and he walked quietly to the front doors of the livery and tested the latch. It lifted and gently he eased open the outer door. Still there was no sound from inside, no restless moving about of horses shifting in their sleep. Carefully, Craig opened the door wider and slipped into the darkness of the building. He saw a rectangle of light ahead and realized that one of the rear doors gaped open. Quickly now, his footfalls muffled by the litter covering the floor, he moved forward to the open doorway.

The alley lay just beyond, ending on Craig's right by turning sharply eastward along a narrow, rutted road that ran parallel to the river. And now he could hear the sounds he had expected before—the sounds of men and of horses.

He walked to the corner of the livery and looked eastward, up the river road. He could see them in the moonlight, a group of men on horseback. They were bunched between the river on their right and a ramshackle house and small barn on their left. For all the brightness of the moonlight, he could only guess at their number. Somewhere between fifteen and twenty, he judged.

He moved ahead softly, his feet seeking dusty soft spots in the road. Now the voices became distinct and the shapes of individual men on horseback began to stand out instead of being no more than a blur against the night.

The sharp, half whining voice of Wallace, the mill owner, came clearly to Craig. "You aren't the law, old man. Not any longer. If you've got any sense, you'll move aside and let us do our job."

"A man doesn't have to wear a badge to stand up against

47

a crazy mob!" Craig heard the tired voice of Frank Fitchen retort. "And that's all you are, whatever name you call yourselves. A mob going after men who can't protect themselves. But give one of them—just one—a gun, and you'd all run like rabbits for your holes!"

And the rumbling, sour tones of Joe Teazel. "You got one minute to get out of the way and then we ride you down, Fitchen!"

Craig put a hand on his gun butt. "And you've got one minute to break this up and get about your business," he said clearly.

Riders reined horses around in surprise. Craig recognized a few of the faces as having been in the crowd at the restaurant earlier. But he dismissed most of them as unimportant. Without their leaders they would be nothing. And the leaders were easy to identify—Wallace and Joe Teazel and the stocky, moustached man that Craig suspected was Riley. They formed a line of three at the front of the group. Some fifteen feet beyond them, planted solidly in the middle of the road, was Frank Fitchen, a carbine in his hands. All of the riders were armed, but Craig noticed that most of them held their guns as if they weren't too sure what to do with them.

No one answered him, nor moved, and he said, "I'm the law here now and there are some new rules. One of them is that nobody carries a gun in town. If he lives here, he leaves it home. If he rides in, he checks it at the jail or at the first place he stops."

"And when did you *put* that rule into effect, marshal?" Wallace asked sarcastically.

"Just after I shot the hat off Cloyd Luvain's head and the gun out of his hand," Craig said evenly. "Just before I made him change his mind about hitting Sangaree tonight."

There was silence again. Craig added, his voice thin, "Do you want a demonstration, gents?"

Some of the men moved, their guns disappearing into holsters or saddle boots or, more commonly, into the belts holding up their trousers. Only the three in the front kept their weapons in the open.

"Luvain's plagued us long enough," Wallace snapped. "This is our chance to get even and we're taking it!"

"Luvain is burying his brother," Craig said quietly. "He and his men are unarmed. I gave them my word they'd be safe tonight. I don't intend to let a brave type like you make a liar out of me."

"And tomorrow night he comes back, and then what?" Teazel demanded.

"Nothing, as long as he behaves himself," Craig said. "Luvain and his men check their guns the same as everyone else."

"And if he doesn't?"

"Then the same thing will happen to him that's going to happen to all of you if you don't obey the law—he'd spend the night in jail and pay a fifty dollar fine to get himself out."

His voice sharpened. "Mr. Fitchen, how many shells do you have?"

"A full load," Fitchen answered.

"That'll do," Craig said, "All right, gents. Let me see your hardware hit the road—all of it. Then ride home. You can come to the jail office and claim your guns tomorrow."

"No, by God!" Teazel blustered.

"Then get ready to spend the night in jail and have your fifty dollars handy tomorrow," Craig said. "Or you can work it out at a dollar a day and found. The town streets need a lot of smoothing for winter."

A man close to Craig said, "Fifty dollars! That's more'n I make in a month." His gun glinted in the moonlight and then thudded to the ground. Others followed until Craig had counted an even dozen pieces of assorted hardware. Most of the other riders began to melt away from them.

"You've got one last chance," Craig said. "Then you'll be adding resisting arrest to the charges." He paused and added, "I killed one man today. I could have killed another. I'm tired and I'm not in any mood for your kind of games. Now drop those guns!"

Fitchen's carbine clicked as he levered a shell into the chamber. It seemed to be the final word. Three guns dropped heavily to the ground. "You haven't heard the last of this!" Wallace said angrily.

Craig ignored him. "Teazel, you'd better round up all the horses you lent out of your livery and then get yourself to bed. The same goes for the rest of you." He walked forward until he was next to Wallace's horse. "Except for you. Get off and walk!"

"Why should I?"

"Because I want your horse to use to haul these guns to the jail office," Craig answered. "You've got a loud mouth so you've probably got good legs."

"Go to hell!"

Craig reached up and in one sudden move plucked Wallace sideways out of the saddle. He caught the man just before he would have sprawled in the dirt. "Take your complaint to the law," Craig said evenly. "Now move along."

The two men still on horseback rode away. Wallace hesitated and then stomped after them. Fitchen came up to Craig. "I handled men that way when I was younger."

Craig began to gather up weapons. "I'd say you did a pretty good job tonight." He looked curiously at the old man. "I misjudged you, Mr. Fitchen. I apologize."

"No need," Fitchen said. "What I was earlier and what I became when I saw that mob forming—they aren't the same thing." He gave a wry smile. "I'm like an old warhorse, I guess. But if there was one thing that put my back up when I was lawing around the country, it was a mob. I can't tolerate 'em—like packs of mindless animals, all following a leader."

Craig managed to load all the guns on the horse or in its saddlebags. He roped them securely. "I didn't come here to take your job, Mr. Fitchen. If you want it back, say the word."

"I figure if I had to do it over again, I'd do the same thing," Fitchen said. "I just decided I was pretty smart, picking you for the job."

Craig caught up the horse's reins. "Clara has pie and coffee waiting, I hear. I'd be obliged if you'd join me."

They went down the alley together, the horse jangling along behind.

VIII

By THE END of Craig's first two weeks as marshal, the weather shifted from late summer to deep fall. A day of thin, cold rain was followed by clear, sunny days and frosty nights, each growing chillier until shards of ice began to rim the backwaters of the river. Now and then a wind coming down from the north promised snow before long, and Craig took to wearing his sheep-fur lined coat on night patrol.

He had given himself the night shift, leaving the daytimes to his deputy. He chuckled a little now as he made his way past the Sangaree House and south across the side street. Choosing Adam Briggs as his assistant had sent a lot of tongues clucking, but he had guessed right, he knew now. The tubby little man with the rusty voice had a rare courage and he was so proud of his star that no job was too much for him to tackle, no hours too long to keep.

More than once, Briggs had hinted he would be willing to take night duty, but Craig kept it for himself, not telling Briggs his reason for doing so. He had faith in the little man but he also was aware of his lack of experience. And although Luvain hadn't appeared in town since the night he had buried his brother and ridden uneventfully away, some of his men occasionally drifted in. At first they'd tried to give Craig trouble about checking their guns, but knocking one down and outdrawing the other had changed their minds quickly enough. Even so, Craig knew, Luvain was not through with Sangaree. And if he came it would most likely be at night, and with trouble in his mind.

Craig's route carried him into the saloons to check for guns and drunks, both forbidden now, but it was a week night and he saw nothing that even hinted of trouble. He continued on, checking dark doorways and thick shadows more out of habit than because he expected to find someone lurking in the darkness. And finally, as always, he ended his swing in front of the building that housed both Marnie's dress shop and Clara's restaurant.

It was past eleven and often at this hour Marnie would still have a light on, showing that she was working at her sewing. At such times, Craig would stop in for late coffee and pie with her and for easy, comfortable talk. Otherwise he went into Clara's, since, without fail, she stayed open until the last saloon customer had taken himself to bed and there was no more hope of selling food.

Tonight Marnie's window was dark and Craig went into the warmth of the little restaurant. Clara was wiping up the counter, readying to close. "I wondered if you'd come in. I saved some coffee and cake."

Craig shucked his coat and hat and slid onto his favorite stool. "I smelled it all the way down to the river," he said. He smiled at her. Despite her habitually sharp voice, he knew there was a fondness in her for him and he returned it.

Clara brought the cake and coffee and poured coffee for herself. "Thackaberry said tonight you were trying to talk the valley and hill ranchers into having a meeting."

"You never miss a thing," Craig commented. He sampled the cake. "In these past two weeks, the nearest thing I've had to trouble has been Kearney," he said. "I talked to Jerrod and we decided that the best thing to do was get the six men together and try to make Kearney and Finch and Truesdale see the truth. I've talked enough to those hill men to know they've got no more to do with Luvain and his kind than you or Marnie. Anyway, I finally got Kearney to agree. And the meeting is set for tomorrow night in the Sangaree House."

"I wish you luck," she said dryly, "but don't expect any. Those valley men want that hill land back. They won't listen to reason. Oh, maybe Truesdale will, but not the other two."

Craig frowned. "What can the three hill men do against the valley ranchers and their crews besides pack up and go?" He shook his head. "It's that or stand and be killed if we don't stop all this."

"I can tell you they won't run," Clara said flatly. "Thackaberry sold a good law practice in North Dakota and came here for his health. He's twice the man he was six months ago. And as for Dwyer and Cardon, they're young and full of beans. And they have all their savings tied up in their places. And with wives and young babies to feed, they'll stand against Kearney and the others."

She drank some coffee and then regarded him with a shake of her head. "You came here two weeks ago, Ben. From your talk, you were going to kill Cloyd Luvain and then ride on. You turned away from your chance to kill him that first night even though you had a right with his shooting at you."

"I was the law by then," Craig said. "I took the job to protect the town from Luvain—in a way his coming was my doing. He'd have had to come a lot closer to killing me than he did for me to kill him as long as I'm the law."

Her smile was thin. "But in two weeks you haven't gone after him. It isn't fear—I know you too well by now to think that. So there's something else."

"You seem to have me all figured out." He laughed. "You tell me what it is."

"You've gone and tied yourself up with people's problems," she said. "There's a compassion in you for other folks. And I'm willing to wager that you'll stay until those problems are solved. That's one thing keeping you here."

"And another?"

"Marnie," she said. Her voice was sharp again. "Now that I've said it, I might as well talk about it. You two have become mighty close in two weeks. You're the only man here she's ever shown an interest in. What happens to her if you kill Cloyd and ride off?"

"Don't try to make too much of a friendship, Clara. Marnie and I like the same things. We both lived on ranches and in cities and so we have a lot to talk about."

Her voice was almost waspish. "I'm twenty years older than Marnie. Her mother died bearing her and I stayed home to raise her. Then our father died. By that time she was old enough to show the talent she has for designing things. I sold the ranch and took her to the city and put her in school. And she did fine. As you well know, she's more than a dressmaker—she's a designer. She made good money working as one in San Francisco. Maybe we should have stayed there but I had my pride and I didn't like her doing all the work and me doing none."

Her voice was softly bitter, self-punishing. "And living in the city didn't agree with me or maybe it was the ocean air. So we went east to Denver. But the same thing happened there. I can't do anything but ranch or cook. What good am I in a city? Then one time Park Jerrod took his wife to Denver to buy new clothes, and we met him. One thing led to another and he suggested we come here and both have little businesses.

"It seemed a fine idea at first, but now I know better. Marnie never complains, but what kind of place is this for a woman of her talent? If she stays, she'll spend her life making dresses for women shaped like bags of flour or she'll marry some small townsman and end with a batch of kids."

"Then sell out and take her back to the city," Craig said.

Clara emptied the coffeepot by pouring the last into their mugs. "Portland is a growing city," she said pointedly. "From what you told me, the land you and your brother own is close there."

Craig swallowed a smile. "A small part is. The rest is farther up the river."

"Well then, you could live in Portland and use the small part to breed those horses you're always talking about and Marnie could design clothes for the society women—have her own salon, even."

"You embarrass a man," Craig said. "Marnie's never shown me she thinks that way about me. And besides, I have no right to think about her like that. Not yet. Because one of these times I'm going to try to kill Cloyd Luvain. But I could get killed instead."

"So you could," she agreed. "But I don't think you will." Her eyes snapped at him. "Keep in mind what I said, Ben. And if you're just using Marnie to keep from being lonesome, stop it. She's too fine a person to be treated so."

"I know that," Craig agreed. Rising, he picked up his coat and hat and started for the door. "I won't hurt her, Clara. Not on purpose. Not if I live."

He went out into the night and started back for his office.

He thought briefly of what Clara had said and then turned his mind to the next night's meeting. He was worrying it when he reached the cross street and glanced eastward. No homes were lighted at this hour and it was easy to see the ridge of the hills behind Jerrod's house. He started as something blotted out the stars there. His eyes watched the shape until he was sure he was actually seeing something. Then it disappeared.

Horse and rider, Craig decided. "Dropped down the ridge," he said aloud. He stood a moment, trying to visualize the ridge in that part of the hills. There was a trail of sorts that followed a dry wash more or less in the direction of town.

If the rider kept on the trail, he would have to pass close to the copse of trees at the edge of town before he could pick up the main road, Craig knew. And if he was a rancher, he'd turn north; if he was a townsman, he'd turn south onto the main street.

But why would anyone, rancher or townsman, ride the ridge at this hour of the night?

Craig hurried his steps now, passing the jail and following the extension of the alley until he reached the copse of trees. He eased into them, settling himself where the trail from the ridge came up out of the wash onto the flat. There was little light, but if he was correct and a horse and rider came into view, he would be able to see them plainly enough.

He heard the sound of hooves on gravel first. Then he saw the horse's head as the animal lurched up a steep, short bank. And finally, he saw the rider.

He watched Cloyd Luvain put the smoke onto the valley road and sink spurs into the horse's flanks, sending it northward at a dead run.

Craig straightened up and turned to go back to town. He asked himself what this could mean. But no matter how many ways he turned it in his mind, he could find no sensible answer.

IX

Jerrod stood in the thick darkness of the windowless rear room of the bank building, his hand resting on his gun butt. With Cloyd Luvain, he thought bitterly, you could take no chances. He wished that he could have found a more predictable man for this work but he had had no choice.

He said now, "What the devil have you been doing for two weeks? The evening Pete was shot you told me you wanted the money in two days. And then you pull that crazy stunt and nearly get yourself killed. You could have ruined everything! And on top of that, you disappear when I need you most."

"Me and the boys had a little job up across the border," Luvain said. "We made some money and we rounded up a few men we can use when the time comes."

Jerrod said thinly, "With Ben Craig after you, Canada was a good place to hide."

"Hell, I ain't afraid of him!" Luvain's voice was loud.

"Keep quiet. Sound carries on this cold air," Jerrod snapped. "Craig's hell on wheels, and you know it. He made a fool out of you. We both know that any time he takes the notion, he can do the same thing to you he did to Pete."

Luvain swore thickly. "Stop pushing me, Jerrod. I came here to talk business and to get the money you owe. Let's get to it."

Jerrod's voice continued to slash at him. "I've heard Craig's story. If I didn't want those valley ranches so badly, I'd kill you myself."

Luvain gave a dry laugh. "But you do want 'em, Jerrod. You're eating yourself up inside hungering for all that land—and for the power it'll give you. And you need me to get what you want. Just remember that."

Jerrod realized the pointlessness of fighting with Luvain. The man was too arrogant to really take orders, even to understand that his position was a menial one. Jerrod said, "All right, now listen closely. We'll have to move soon—before the snow comes to stay. I've got it figured out this way: we make two moves—one the night after tomorrow—

that'll stir the valley ranchers against the hill men. But not a big hit. I just want Kearney and the others to simmer; I don't want them to blow up yet."

"Why all the fooling around?" Luvain demanded.

"I'm going to use that hit to try to make Craig marshal of the whole Sangaree, not just the town."

"That means he'll be marshal as far as Goldbar! By God, if he comes to my town, I'll have a dozen men waiting to put lead in him."

"Don't be a fool," Jerrod snapped. "I want to use him, not kill him—not right away. When you make the big hit, he'll have to be there as the law. . ."

"We planned it all out that day Pete was killed," Luvain interrupted. He sounded impatient now. "I'll make the hit right after midnight and it'll be the way you want it. Now give me the money and then you can go home to that pretty wife of yours. The boys are getting impatient for their gold."

Reluctantly, Jerrod reached beside him and lifted a sack of gold coins. They represented money deposited by the townspeople. Then he shrugged. What difference did it make? Before there was a chance of the shortage being discovered, he would own the valley as well as the town. All he had to do then would be sell off a few head of stock and have the money to return to the bank.

He tossed the sack in the general direction he thought Luvain to be. "Here."

The sack thudded to the floor and then the coins clinked as Luvain found them. "This better be right," he said.

"It's right. Now get out of here. Craig is always with Marnie Clayton or in the restaurant at this time. That'll give you a chance to get out of town without being seen and me to get to the hotel."

"Hotel?" Luvain echoed. "I thought you were going home."

"Not tonight. I have too much to do setting up a meeting between the ranchers and the hill men for tomorrow." Jerrod stifled a yawn. "Besides, I'm tired. Now ride."

With a soft grunt that sounded almost pleased, Luvain eased to the door and lifted the latch. He opened it cautiously and glanced into the alley that ran behind the bank. It was empty and he hurried out and into darkness. His horse was in the copse of trees at the edge of town and he worked his way to it, keeping in shadow. Once, when he had an angle view of the front of the Sangaree House, he stopped and watched Jerrod going inside. After a moment, lamplight showed through the near window of Jerrod's suite. Luvain made a pleased sound and hurried his pace.

A dry wash coming down from the east hills ended at the edge of the stand of trees. Luvain put his horse down into the wash and trotted it quickly up into the hills and onto the crest of the first ridge. Here he turned south and worked his way to a point directly above the last house on Sangaree's one main cross street. It was a big, rambling building, set behind a high wall. A stand of scrub timber ran patchily from the ridge to the east side of the wall and Luvain used the shadows it cast to work his way downslope. Leaving the horse, he eased along the wall to the rear corner and slipped through a small gate into a garden. Directly ahead of him was a many-windowed sunroom. He walked openly toward it, not concerned about the Jerrods' servants since they slept above the stable on the far side of the big house.

Luvain stopped by a closed window and tapped lightly on the glass. A moment of silence hung on the chilly night. Then he heard a rustling sound followed by footsteps. The window latch was released. Luvain slid the sash up and climbed into a warm room, fragrant with the scent Anita Jerrod used. She stood a few feet away, misty in white.

"He's staying at the hotel?"

"So he said," Luvain answered. He remained where he was, making her come to him to be kissed. When he had finished, she drew away, shivering a little.

"It's been so long. Almost a month since I've seen you alone." With a soft cry, she kissed him again, hungrily. "Talk to me," she whispered as she moved back. "I've almost forgotten how much like home your voice is."

"Talk!" he said scornfully, and pulled her against him.

When he stood again at the window, ready to leave, she said, "Cloyd, be careful of that man Craig. I heard what he did to you the night you buried Pete. And I saw

58

him—shoot Pete. Please don't fight him again. Promise me you won't."

"I'll fight him again," Luvain said. "But this time I'll know what to do. And it won't be Craig who puts a bullet in me."

"Everyone knows that you're brave and dangerous. You don't have to keep proving it!"

"Listen," he said savagely, "Craig killed Pete. He's going to pay for that. Besides, I want him out of the way. I got plans—like I told you before. One of these days I'm going to be as big a man here as that husband of yours. And when I am, then I'm going to have you along with everything else!"

"Is that why you fought Park—because of me? Is that why you tried to have Pete beat him up?"

"That was business. But don't worry. It won't happen again. Him and me are as good as partners right now. So stop fretting."

She said in a soft, worrying way, "You say you'll have me, but Park will never give me up. And I owe him too much to feel right about leaving him."

"You let me take care of it," he boasted.

"I love you," she whispered.

He kissed her again and then slipped outside and hurried back to his horse. From a point on the ridge trail, he could look down on the town and see the light burning in the jail building. He shook his fist at it. "You may be tough, Craig, but you ain't tough enough. You'll learn that when you're dying slow with my bullet in your belly!" Kicking his horse into action, he sent it down into the dry wash and back toward the stand of trees.

X

WITHIN five minutes of the beginning of the meeting, Craig knew that it was going to be a waste of time. Within a half hour, he realized that trouble was coming sooner or later, and he could think of no way to turn it aside.

Jerrod sat close to Craig at one end of the parlor of his hotel suite. At an angle to their left sat the valley ranchers—

Kearney and Finch, big, solid men with arrogance even in the way they lounged in their chairs, and Truesdale, younger and seemingly a little more open-minded. Near them sat Tip Fraley, Finch's foreman, and Arty Logan, brought by Kearney as a witness.

Directly opposite the valley men the three hill ranchers clustered together—Dwyer and Cardon, young and a bit awed by the opulence of their surroundings, and Thackaberry, older and completely at his ease.

Craig said, "The first night I came here, I heard Kearney accuse Thackaberry of stealing valley stock. I've heard it a lot since then, but no one's offered any proof."

"What do you call proof?" Kearney rumbled. "Tip Fraley found a dozen head wearing our brands mixed with theirs and being drifted north. That was about two months ago. A week later Truesdale trailed some of his stock into a big canyon that cuts through the west hills and ends up across the border. Whoever was pushing 'em heard him coming and got out of sight. The weather'd been wet and there was a good set of prints made by a horse with a broken shoe on his off hind hoof. The next day Truesdale found Cardon here replacing a broken shoe on the off hind foot of one of his horses."

He snorted. "I can give you a half dozen more pieces of proof just like those. How much do you want?"

"Circumstantial evidence, all of it," Thackaberry said in his lawyer's voice. "Both Dwyer and I told you again and again that we had nothing to do with putting your stock in with ours. And the one time you found him with the cattle, he was trying to sort yours out and put them back on the summer range where they'd been. As for Cardon, he told Truesdale that his horse had disappeared two days before and then come wandering back. It happens. You know that."

"All I know," Kearney said in his heavy, stubborn way, "is that when roundup is finished this fall, I'll be short close to thirty head. And Finch and Truesdale maybe even more. I didn't raise that beef to support squatters with."

"I've lost stock too," Jerrod reminded them. "But I prefer to keep an open mind until I actually catch one of the hill men stealing."

"You would," Kearney grunted. "You brought the three of them here. You set 'em up in business and I suspect you're still buying half their groceries even yet. Besides, ever since you fired the Luvains, you want to blame everything on them."

"You got to admit they probably have a hand in it," Finch said. "The way I figure, the hill men pick off our stock that's up on summer grass, run it to those so-called miners at Goldbar and let them push it across the border and sell it for them." He pushed his big jaw out belligerently. "If it isn't that way, why don't these squatters lose any of their beef? Why is it always us alone?"

"I admit it sounds that way," Truesdale said carefully, "but I tend to agree with Jerrod here. Until we catch them in the act, we have no real evidence."

They kept hammering at it until finally Kearney got up, disgust deep on his face. "Unless somebody's got something to say worth listening to, I'm going to have me a drink and ride home." He stabbed a finger at the three hill ranchers. "And I ain't waiting for the time when I catch you three in the act." He snorted. "Hell, with a man like Thackaberry here telling you other two what to do, I don't figure to catch you out. He's too smart for that."

"The good Lord himself couldn't open Kearney's eyes," Thackaberry commented quietly.

"I'm not waiting for him neither," Kearney said. "The next time I find any of my stock in with any of yours, the next time anything happens that isn't natural—then I'm coming after you three." He looked at Finch and Truesdale. "I figure that the three of us can rake up men enough to send you packing back to where you came from."

"And if they don't go?" Craig asked softly.

"We got a few men that know how to handle guns too," Kearney said.

Jerrod stood up. "Before you go charging around like a wild bull, Kearney, listen to a suggestion. Make a real effort to find out the truth. And if the hill ranchers are rustling your stock, make them pay for it legally—by going to jail. If it's Luvain and his crew, then have them jailed."

He took a step forward. "I'm suggesting that we extend

Craig's jurisdiction to cover the whole Sangaree—and let him do the job of finding out what is actually happening."

"I've been my own law for twenty years," Kearney snapped. "I'm not about to have Craig here or anyone else snoop around my place and tell me that me and my men can't wear guns on my own land!"

"Don't be a fool," Jerrod answered. "That gun law applies to the town and nowhere else. It's here for the same reason Craig put in the law that says barkeeps can't sell a man too much liquor—to stop trouble before it starts."

"I have to admit I have more men able to work after a night in town than I did before," Truesdale remarked.

Kearney gave one of his heavy snorts. "The devil with all this! I gave my warning." He jerked open the door and stalked out. Finch rose to follow. Truesdale stood up as well.

He said, "It's worth thinking over." With a nod, he followed Finch out.

"I was hoping for more from this meeting," Thackaberry said.

"It will take more than words to change a bullheaded mind like Kearney's," Jerrod said. "And Finch always goes the way Kearney goes. I'd say your best chance is to go home and pray for a miracle."

"You'd be wiser to go home and load your guns," Craig said.

"So I was thinking," Dwyer said with surprising strength. Cardon nodded agreement and then with Thackaberry behind them, the pair left. Thackaberry turned in the doorway.

"Thank you for your efforts, gentlemen. Good night."

As the door closed, Jerrod raised both hands. "Unless something happens to make Kearney see things differently, we're going to have a range war on our hands." He looked closely at Craig. "What will you do then, marshal?"

"If it stays in the valley, it won't be the law's affair," Craig pointed out. "But if the odds are too great, I'd probably resign my job and throw in with the hill men. I don't like bullying, and that's what Kearney is doing. I get the feeling he wants his free grass back and he won't be satisfied until he gets it."

"I wouldn't argue that," Jerrod said. He nodded a good night as Craig went to the door.

Tiredly, Craig crossed to the jail office and told Adam Briggs to go get some sleep. "Tomorrow is Saturday and we'll both be working late," he said.

Briggs' glance was shrewd. "I see you got nowhere with Kearney. I didn't expect you to."

"I didn't either," Craig admitted. "But it was worth trying."

Briggs readied himself to leave. "Any more ideas, marshal?"

"One," Craig said. He nodded good night and went out and down the street to the restaurant. At this hour, he expected to find Frank Fitchen there, having his final cup of coffee before going to his lonely room and bed. The place was crowded with families but there was an empty stool beside the one Fitchen occupied. Craig slid onto it.

"I'd like some advice, if you have time," he said quietly.

The old man's eyes showed pleasure. "Glad to." He finished his coffee and stood up. "In your office?"

"That'll be fine," Craig said. He rose too. "Save me some of that beefsteak, Clara," he said, and followed Fitchen outside.

In his office, Craig found the coffee still hot in its pot on the stove. He poured two mugs and handed one to Fitchen. Then he sat down and began packing his pipe. He said bluntly, "Last night late I saw somebody on the ridge above Jerrod's house. It was Cloyd Luvain. But Jerrod himself spent the night in the hotel."

"You was bound to find out sooner or later," Fitchen said. "I just hope Jerrod never hears—nor any of the windy gossips in this town."

"You're trying to tell me that Luvain is visiting Mrs. Jerrod?"

"I just did tell you," the old man said. He sipped his coffee. "I don't hold no brief for Cloyd Luvain, God knows, but I hold less for Jerrod where that wife of his is concerned. When I first found out, I was pretty upset. I couldn't figure out what a pretty, well raised lady like her would be taking up with the likes of Luvain for."

He made a wry face. "I even braced Luvain about it. Without coming out and admitting anything, he made it

63

pretty clear to me that if the word ever got around, I'd be the first man he'd shoot. But that ain't why I never spoke up. I got to thinking and I realized you couldn't blame Mrs. Jerrod much. Nor Luvain, for that matter. He's more or less human and I suspect she started it when he was working on Jerrod's ranch."

Craig sat quietly, smoking and drinking his coffee, letting Finch tell the story his own way. The old man said, "She was raised to a lot of money when she was real young. Then the war came and like a lot of Southern folks, she spent some of her time being hungry. Jerrod met her one time when he was in New Orleans and he married her. I don't figure he really loves her or ever did, but she was the prettiest thing he'd ever seen and he wanted her to show off with—the same way he built the Sangaree House, to let folks know how big and rich a man he is.

"Anyway, he brought her here and for all that he was obviously showing her off the way he would a prize filly, she tried hard to live up to her part of the bargain and make a good wife for the most important man in the Sangaree. But after a while, he as good as forgot her. And he's too busy with his own affairs to concern himself with her happiness.

"And then she's Deep South and so is Cloyd, even if they ain't the same kind of South. Jerrod, he's East." He shook his head. "If you'd seen Mrs. Jerrod riding these hills day after day, in all kinds of weather—just so she'd have something to do with her time—you'd know better what I mean. Why, I'll bet odds that she knows the east hills better'n anyone else in these parts, she's ridden 'em so much."

"Still," Craig said, "she was with Jerrod that day on the pass."

"Maybe they rode together—once in a while he'd let her help him hunt strays—and maybe Cloyd told her to take herself a ride and be at the saloon at a certain time. That'd be like him, wanting to have her watch while Pete beat up her husband."

He sighed. "With it all, I still get the feeling she thinks a lot of Jerrod. Maybe she even still loves him. But she's as human as the rest of us, and being lonesome can eat you up pretty bad."

"I know," Craig said quietly. He saw the worry on Fitchen's face and took it away quickly. "My interest is in Luvain, not Mrs. Jerrod. You don't have to worry about my trotting to her husband with the story."

Fitchen rose. "I like her," he said. "I wouldn't want to see her get hurt."

"If she stays tied to Luvain, she's likely to," Craig said.

"So she is. I wish I knew a way to tell her."

"Does Luvain go there often?"

"Sometimes he seems to know when Jerrod is staying at the hotel—like most Saturday nights. That's when I've seen him there most often. Otherwise, I couldn't say."

He left then and Craig went back to the restaurant for his supper. Most of the crowd had gone and by the time he was finished, he was alone with the two women. Clara retired to the kitchen to wash dishes, leaving him with Marnie for company.

"How did the meeting go, Ben?"

He made a sour face. "Like you'd expect with Kearney there." He sketched out for her what had happened.

"What if they'd agreed to let you be the law in the Sangaree? Would you have taken the job?"

"If it might stop a range war, yes."

"But as the law, you'd be tied more than you are now as far as killing Cloyd Luvain is concerned," she pointed out.

"I already figured that out," he admitted. He looked into Marnie's smoky eyes. "I had a talk with Clara last night. She pointed out to me how I've kept off killing Cloyd and taking on other folks' troubles. She told me why too."

They both laughed softly and then, suddenly, they were no longer laughing but looking full at one another. "Was she right, Ben?"

"She was right," Craig admitted. "She said—in a way—that I'm a kind of busybody when it comes to other people."

"Was that the only reason?"

"No," he said softly. "The other reason is you."

"I could have told you that a week ago," Marnie whispered softly.

"It's nothing I have a right to talk about, things being as they are."

"I'm a grown woman," she said. "I know the risks I'm taking, letting myself feel as I do." Her voice thinned out. "Don't make me feel you're setting aside your promise to Chalco because of me."

"No," Craig said. "Sooner or later, I'm going to try. And I get the feeling it won't be long now."

XI

CRAIG SQUATTED in deep shadow at the upper end of the line of scrub trees that ran downslope to the wall around Jerrod's house. He could see Luvain's big smoky horse standing patiently where its owner had tied it, and he wondered if the animal was growing as tired and cold as he was.

This was not the kind of work Craig enjoyed. Spying had never been to his taste, whatever the reason for it. But after his talk with Fitchen last night, he had known he would be here—he couldn't pass up the chance to give Luvain a final warning. And as Fitchen had predicted, Luvain had come this night, Saturday, although so early after the first deep darkness that Craig had almost been caught off guard. But his frequent inspection of the ridge of the east hills had paid its dividend and he had seen the telltale blotting out of the stars not a half hour before.

Craig had followed Luvain's route up the dry wash to the ridge and along it to the top of the stand of trees above the walled-in house. At first, he thought of going to the house and accosting Luvain there. He decided against it, not wanting to embarrass Anita Jerrod. At the same time he rejected trying to slip close enough to eavesdrop, the thought of it too galling to his nature.

Instead, he satisfied himself with slipping down the hill and leading Luvain's horse back into the clump of shadow where he had been squatting. To his surprise, Luvain came into view almost before Craig had settled back on his heels. He barely had time to slip Luvain's carbine from its boot,

66

empty out the shells, and replace the gun before Luvain discovered that his horse was missing.

Craig watched with pleasure as Luvain's puzzlement turned to anger. Finally Luvain struck a match and bent, seeking sign on the hard ground. Since Craig had carefully led the horse where its hoof-marks would show in disturbed pine needles, Luvain was not long in starting up the slope on foot. As he neared, Craig could hear him cursing all wandering animals.

With less than six feet separating them, Craig said softly, "Your horse is here, Luvain, with me."

Luvain went into a half crouch, his hand slapping for the gun at his hip. Craig's voice froze him, the gun still in its holster. "Don't be a fool. You clear leather and I'll have a hole through you."

Luvain straightened up. "Craig, by God!" he whispered. "So Jerrod finally found out and sent you here to do his dirty work!"

"If Jerrod knew, he'd be here himself," Craig said. "And he wouldn't have given you warning—he'd have shot first."

"He doesn't give a hang for his wife!"

"Maybe not, but he does for himself and for the way other folks see him."

Luvain waved the argument aside. "What do you want, Craig? To kill me? Is that why you're here, then?"

"In Sangaree I'm the law, not an executioner," Craig answered. "I'm here to give you two warnings, Luvain: keep away from Mrs. Jerrod. In five years I've seen everything you've touched turn rotten. She deserves better than you."

"Ask her how she feels."

There was no fear in the man, Craig thought. He might be careful, always trying to make sure he had the long end of the odds, but he was no coward. Craig said, "And second, keep your hands off valley beef."

"Shucks, marshal, I thought you were going to say you'd run to Jerrod and tattle on me," Luvain mocked.

"Your horse is over to your left. Get on him and ride!" Craig snapped.

Laughing, Luvain mounted and rode upslope and turned north. But once beyond Craig's hearing the laughter died.

How the devil had Craig found out about his visits here? And just what would Craig do about them? Luvain had no intention of giving up his trips to see Anita Jerrod because of a warning. He thought back to the time he'd learned that old fool Fitchen had known about him and Anita. Without putting a threat into plain words, he had scared the marshal badly enough to be sure Fitchen would keep his mouth shut.

He smashed the flat of his hand down on his thigh. That's what he'd do with Craig. It was still early. The raid on the valley wasn't to take place until after midnight. That gave him plenty of time to let Craig know just where he stood with Cloyd Luvain. He'd whip Craig in front of the very people Craig had been bullying with his crazy laws about no guns and no drunks. Then Craig would see how much weight he carried as marshal. And at the same time, Luvain thought, he'd be giving Craig the same kind of warning he'd given Fitchen.

Luvain chuckled. What was more, Jerrod would praise him—because he'd tell Jerrod he was just making sure that Craig didn't interfere in the night's business.

Now he turned the horse downslope and cantered it through the dry wash and onto the road by the trees at the edge of town. But instead of turning north, he reined south and pushed the horse down the main street. Outside of Jerrod's fancy saloon in the hotel, the biggest place in town was Sharkey's—which, Luvain thought with a chuckle, belonged appropriately enough to Jerrod himself.

The hitching rail before the saloon was lined with horses. Luvain tied his own mount and walked in. It was full, with the small dance floor taken up by five stomping cowhands and the saloon's complement of local dancing girls.

Sharkey, behind the bar, called, "Check your gun here, Cloyd."

"Where I go, my gun goes," Luvain answered. He elbowed his way to the bar. "Give me a drink."

The piano player's hands slid off the keys, the dancers stopped their gyrations, and the sounds that had filled the room dribbled away. Everyone was watching the bar now.

Sharkey said, "Sure." He reached down for a bottle and

when he came up, there was a gun in his hand. "Check your gun, Cloyd—now."

Luvain stared insolently at him. "Let the law tell me."

Sharkey held the gun steady. "One of you boys run up to the jail and bring the marshal. Tell him he's got his first customer in quite a spell."

"Give me that drink while we're waiting," Luvain said.

Craig grunted, understanding the meaning of this. He stepped down from the paint and tied it in front of the restaurant. Then he walked on down to the saloon and inside. The men closest to Luvain melted away, leaving him standing alone, a glass of whiskey in one huge hand.

"The law says check your gun," Craig said quietly. "Give it over."

Luvain downed his whiskey. "And let you shoot me, marshal? I ain't that crazy!"

Now Craig was sure he had been right a moment ago— this was Luvain's answer to being caught up at the Jerrod house. He was going to try to do to Craig what he had more than once done to. Fitchen—make a public fool of him.

"Five seconds, or you spend the night in jail."

Luvain took a step forward. "You ain't man enough to put me in jail!" He drew, but so slowly and clumsily that it was obvious he wanted Craig to throw down on him. Craig did, without hurry.

"I say you ain't man enough without that gun in your hand!"

Craig shrugged. "Unbuckle your gunbelt and toss it to Sharkey," he commanded.

Luvain met his gaze and then his own eyes slid away. He was obviously fighting a desire to grin in triumph as he followed Craig's orders. The saloon remained thick with silence. There was no sound but the clatter of Luvain's gun and belt as they landed on the bar beside Sharkey and then the shuffle of his bootsoles as he moved a step forward.

Craig unbuckled his own belt and walked to the bar. He handed the belt to Sharkey and stepped back, moving easily, showing nothing by his expression.

Luvain licked his lips. Craig said, "This is what you wanted, Luvain. Now come and get it."

Luvain came, throwing thirty pounds more than Craig owned in a wild charge. Craig waited until Luvain was almost on him, surprised at the man's lack of finesse, and at the same time noting the solidity of the flesh on the big-boned frame and the easy grace with which Luvain moved all of his weight.

Luvain drew back a fist and started to drive it forward. Craig stepped easily aside and flicked out with twisting knuckles. There was a grunt from the crowd as Luvain, instead of going on past Craig, pivoted like a dancer and turned what had looked like a wildly swinging blow into a deadly weapon aimed straight for Craig's middle.

Craig felt the solid impact of Luvain's rock-hard knuckles. He went off balance, knowing that he was hurt. He tried to catch himself but, arms flailing, he stumbled backward. He crashed into the first row of tables, sending poker chips and cards flying. The table splintered under his weight and the force of his fall and he dropped down in its wreckage.

Luvain pulled his lips back from his teeth in a grin of triumph. He stomped slowly toward Craig, his disdain obvious in the slowness of his movements.

Someone cried from the rear of the room, "Watch out, marshal. He's going to stomp you!" Craig had no need for the warning cry. Luvain's intent was obvious from the eager glow in his eyes.

With an effort that brought the sweat out on his body, Craig managed to free himself from the wrecked table and get to one knee. He slumped that way, head hanging, mouth open, as though he were still unable to find wind or strength enough to make it the rest of the way to his feet. He shook his head as if his eyesight were blurred.

But when Luvain's great boot shot out for his face, Craig leaned aside with a sudden move, reached out with both arms and put his hands on Luvain's ankle. He jerked hard backward, at the same time throwing Luvain's leg up with all the strength he could bring to bear.

With a grunt of surprise, Luvain went backward. He

70

landed on the floor with a thud that sent dust spurting. He rolled and came to his feet with the ease and grace of a trained bear, shaking his head.

But now Craig was on his feet, waiting. He lashed out and caught Luvain a deceptively light blow on the cheekbones. Luvain curled his lips in a sneer and took a step forward, ramming a massive fist at Craig's face. Craig sidestepped and flicked another blow at Luvain's face. Again Luvain came in, but half circling before he swung at Craig.

Craig's expression was impassive, telling Luvain nothing of what went on in his mind. But Luvain could not repress the tight, half contemptuous grin twisting his mouth, since each time Craig hit him and backpedaled, Craig was getting closer and closer to the bar.

This, Craig knew, was Luvain's plan—let him maneuver himself against the bar where Luvain could use his greater weight to pin him and then batter him insensible. And to get Craig in that position, Luvain was obviously willing to take what seemed to be Craig's feather-light fists against his face. Without seeming to understand, Craig continued to be satisfied with his quick, short jabs into Luvain's face.

The room was silent now. If anyone noticed that Luvain's face was beginning to puff up around the eyes from Craig's fists, he said nothing. Only the sound of scuffling feet, of heavy breathing, of knuckles smashing flesh broke the quiet.

XII

CRAIG let a grunt of mixed surprise and pain come out of him as his back came suddenly up against the edge of the bar. He turned his head as if seeking the best way of escape. Luvain was almost on top of him and now Luvain shouted his triumph and drove his great weight forward.

Craig moved with startling speed, dropping down and ducking under Luvain's charge. One great fist came smashing down on the bar top, bringing a howl of pain from Luvain. He turned to find Craig in front of him and his own back to the bar.

And now there was no more lightness to Craig's blows.

71

His fists slashed into Luvain's face, twisting and cutting the already puffed flesh. Blood spurted from Luvain's smashed nose, from lips cut by hard knuckles smashing them against his teeth. He pawed at one eye as he tried to see from between the swellings enclosing it.

Luvain lashed half blindly at Craig. Dancing back, Craig moved quickly in and drummed against Luvain's body. He was seeking a soft spot. But Luvain's belly was corrugated steel. Craig raised his sights and hit Luvain hard under the heart. He saw the color drain from Luvain's face and the heavier man slammed back against the bar edge.

Craig hit him under the heart again and then slashed at his face with two cutting fists. Luvain managed one wild swing that caught Craig on the side of the neck and sent him sprawling. But when he rose, Luvain was still where he had been, fighting to keep himself upright by using the bar as a prop.

Craig walked up to him and deliberately hit him twice more over the heart. Then he stepped back and stood with his arms hanging. Luvain tottered, grasped feebly behind him for support, missed, and then crashed forward. He made a final effort to rise and succeeded only in rolling onto his back. He lay with swollen, almost sightless eyes staring at the ceiling, with blood dribbling from the corners of his open, gasping mouth.

Craig walked to the bar and held out his hand. Sharkey gave him his gun and belt. He buckled them on and looked around at the crowd.

"The law was made for every man who comes to Sangaree." His eyes fastened on Jenks and Shorty, who were standing at the far end of the bar. "Remind your boss of that when he's able to hear you."

He motioned to both men. "Pack him on his horse," he said.

"You running him out of town, marshal?" someone called.

"I'm running him into a jail cell," Craig snapped. He got Luvain's gun and belt from Sharkey and followed Shorty and Jenks out as they packed Luvain's sagging body between them into the chill night air. Luvain stirred against the cold but that was all. With all their strength, Jenks and

Shorty managed to get Luvain belly-down in his saddle.

Craig said, "One of you lead the horse up to the jail. The other one go get Doc Yates and bring him there." Not looking at the crowd that had followed from the saloon, he walked alongside Jenks, leading the horse. Shorty climbed aboard his own animal and rode quickly to the cross street and eastward to the doctor's house.

Briggs stared with wide eyes as between them, Craig and Jenks dragged Luvain into a cell. Except for a red spot on his neck, Craig seemed unmarked.

"Coffee hot?" Craig asked. He dumped Luvain's gun and belt on the desk and reached for his pipe. When Briggs shook his head, Craig said, "Then brew up some. Doc Yates will be along, and Luvain will need something hot when he comes around."

"The doc ain't coming for you?" Briggs sounded worried.

Craig stuffed his pipe carefully. "Luvain got me a few good ones in the body, but I've been bruised worse breaking a horse." He looked at Jenks. "You and your partner might as well ride. Luvain isn't going anyplace tonight."

"We'll go his bail!" Jenks argued. "As soon as the doc fixes him up, we'll go his bail and take him with us."

"When the judge sets bail, then you can go it," Craig said. "Now get riding."

Briggs went to the window as Jenks stomped out. "He's heading hell for leather for the hotel, marshal." He chuckled. "To roust out the judge, I expect."

"He won't get far with Jerrod," Craig observed. He dropped into the chair, aware suddenly of the pain left in his body from Luvain's powerful blows. He watched Briggs bustle around, making the coffee. It was beginning to boil by the time Doctor Yates came into the small room.

Craig unlocked the cell door and waved the doctor in to where Luvain lay breathing thickly. "He's a bull. I don't think he's too badly hurt, but I'd feel better if you'd check him."

Yates was a spare man reaching middle age gracefully. He wasted no time in questions but pulled a chair alongside Luvain's bunk, opened his medical bag, and went to work.

73

When he was finished, Luvain was stirring, showing signs of coming around.

The doctor backed out of the cell and let Craig slam the door shut. "Shorty tells me you had Luvain helpless," he observed. "You could have smashed him worse than you did. You could have broken his face up and blinded him."

"I was doing my job," Craig said. "He broke the law. I ordered him to jail and he refused. So I did what I had to do to get him here."

Briggs said, "The coffee's ready."

"Pass it around, and see if Luvain's ready for some," Craig told him.

Doc Yates shook his head. "If Luvain had had you in the same position, he wouldn't have eased up."

"Luvain isn't the law here," Craig said. "I am. If I abuse my authority, then I've failed in my job. When I kill Luvain, it will be in a fair fight—with bullets—but it won't be where I have the power of my badge behind me."

The doctor took a mug of coffee and blew on it gently. "Clara Clayton told me that's the way you'd think. I wasn't sure she was right—until now."

Craig smiled. "Clara's almost too busy digging into my mind to keep her own on her work."

The smile went away as Jerrod came into the room, followed by Jenks and Shorty. He nodded to Craig and the doctor and then went to the cell and looked in at Luvain. He was sitting up now, holding a mug of hot coffee between his huge hands. One eye was still half swollen shut but the other one was clear. His expression was sullen, almost defiant, as he stared back at Jerrod.

"Name my fine, judge, and let me out of this stinking hole."

Jerrod looked at Craig. "What made you do this to him?" he demanded testily.

Jerrod's attitude surprised Craig. He took a deep puff on his pipe before he said, "Go ask at Sharkey's. They'll tell you what happened."

Jerrod continued to sound irritable, unaccountably so to Craig. "Marshal, I'm trying to find out what the charge against Luvain is. I can't determine his fine or—if he pre-

74

fers to stand trial—set his bail until I know that charge."

"You came over tonight for that?" Craig asked. "Let him cure a little here. He'll keep until morning." He saw Jerrod about to speak and shrugged. "The charge is refusing to check his gun and resisting arrest. The fines on the two charges add up to one hundred and fifty dollars—and two weeks in jail on top of it for resisting arrest."

"You won't keep me in your jail for no two weeks!" Cloyd Luvain cried thickly.

"You have the right to ask for a trial and post bail," Jerrod said quickly. "I'll set that at one hundred dollars."

"This is a farce," Craig snapped. "What defense can he put up when he does come to trial?"

"You're the marshal, not a judge and a jury," Jerrod retorted. "Until you are, do your part in administering the law and leave my part to me."

Craig shrugged again and leaned back in his chair, smoking and sipping his coffee while Shorty, Jenks, and Luvain among themselves disgorged a hundred dollars. Jerrod wrote a formal receipt and handed it through the bars to Luvain.

"Release the prisoner, marshal."

Craig picked up Luvain's gun, emptied it of bullets and returned it to the holster. Then he opened the cell and tossed the gun and belt in to Luvain. Still saying nothing, he returned to his chair.

Luvain walked out slowly. He stopped once to glare at Craig. "You ain't heard the last from me," he said. Then he went out, Shorty and Jenks on either side of him.

Craig remained where he was until the clatter of hooves told him that the three men had ridden north. Slowly, he noticed. Luvain's body wouldn't be up to much jouncing for a while.

The doctor set down his empty coffee mug. "Do you need looking at, marshal?"

"No," Craig said. "Thanks for coming, Doc. Send your bill to the City Clerk."

The doctor nodded, took his bag, and left. Jerrod remained. Craig said, "Briggs, can you make a tour of the town about now?"

The little man nodded and waddled off. Craig looked sourly at Jerrod. "Being a judge is your affair, but it's going to cause talk, your coming over at this time of night just to set bail for Luvain. Most men would have to wait until morning—or even until Monday."

"Use your head," Jerrod snapped. Then his voice gentled. "Look at it sensibly, Craig. Jailing Luvain was one thing—that accomplished your purpose. Everyone in town knows you came here to kill him, but when you had the chance, you didn't take it. That gives the law meaning.

"But letting him stay in jail is something else. He has a dozen or more men probably drunk or well on their way up at Goldbar. All it would take to set off an attack would be for Shorty or Jenks to go riding up there and tell those hardcases that Luvain is in a cell. Not that you couldn't handle another attack on Sangaree, but why bring one down on us at all? Sooner or later I'd have to give Luvain the same privileges as any other man and let him post bail. I just did it tonight to save possible trouble."

"All right," Craig said. "When people ask why Luvain gets special treatment, I'll run them to you for the answer." He picked up his mug and finished his coffee.

Setting the mug on the desk top, he said thoughtfully, "If I'd been that badly beaten, I wouldn't have looked forward to a two hour ride on a cold night. I'd have waited until morning, after I'd slept off some of the pain and soreness."

"Maybe Luvain couldn't stand the thought of spending the night this close to you," Jerrod said lightly. With a nod, he turned and walked out.

Maybe not, Craig agreed, but it was far from a satisfactory explanation. He leaned back, puffing on his pipe and letting his mind work on the problem. Shorty had been so eager to get Luvain away from the jail that he'd dared interrupt Jerrod's Saturday night. And Luvain had obviously been just as eager to go, despite his beating.

Craig pulled himself slowly out of his chair, wincing at the soreness across his ribs. He scribbled a brief note to Briggs and then went out and across to the hotel stable where he kept his horse.

He might be wasting his time, but five years of trailing Luvain had given him almost a sixth sense about the man. Saddling his horse, Craig automatically checked his carbine, put it back in the boot, and then rode outside and down the alley. He cut across to the main street and reined the paint north. At the edge of town, his heels digging into the horse's flanks sent it hurtling forward through the cold night.

XIII

ONCE THE PAINT had the kinks out of its muscles, Craig pushed it to its limit. The road here ran along the edge of the valley, where the almost board-flat floor met the first rise of the eastern hills. Summer's weather had left it in fine shape, smooth for easy riding, and the paint ate up the ground quickly.

At intervals, roads took off—the first to the left to Kearney's big ranch; the second to the right, up the slope to Thackaberry's place; and beyond them, the roads leading to the other valley ranches and to Dwyer's small hill spread. Shortly past the road leading to Thackaberry's, the hills fell away, giving Craig a view straight northward for some distance. He reined in the paint as he saw the dark blotches marking riders up ahead.

He walked the paint now, studying the group still well in front of him. Finally he was able to make out three horses and three riders, and he chuckled sourly. Luvain was taking it slow, he thought. Craig hadn't expected to catch up with the trio until they were well over halfway to the end of the valley.

Then, suddenly, they disappeared. Craig stared intently into the darkness ahead. Had the road curved abruptly? But the hills were still a good hundred yards to the east, giving the road no reason to bend. A thin stand of trees lay ahead where a creek came down to work its way to the river but Luvain and his men would have passed through the trees and back into view within minutes. Yet the longer Craig looked, the emptier the road became.

He reached the trees and clattered softly over a small bridge spanning the creek. He stopped suddenly, understanding now. Running off to Craig's right and following close to the line of willows on the creekbank was a narrow but obviously much used wagonroad. When it reached the hills, it twisted up and went quickly out of sight. It was, Craig recalled from the map Jerrod had given him of the Sangaree, the road to Dwyer's place. And it was the only way Luvain and his men could have gone.

Craig rode carefully now, not wanting the paint to be heard, nor to round a bend and come too quickly on waiting men. Eyes alert for signs of movement ahead, he put his mind to recalling the way this country lay according to Jerrod's detailed map. Dwyer's place was at the foot of a ridge—the same ridge, in fact, that ran behind Jerrod's town house. The road to Dwyer's was originally a cattle trail, used by the valley ranchers to run their beef to summer grass. As a result, a number of narrow trails took off from it, some below Dwyer's and leading into small hollows where the snow left early and grass came on rich and strong in the spring, others higher in the hills and going on to the true mountain meadows.

Craig passed two of the narrow trails and then twisted up a short switchback and came out on a flat bench. At the back side of the bench, huddled under the lee of the rising hills, he could make out the small clump of dark buildings that marked Dwyer's home ranch. As he watched, a light bobbed in the blackness and was swallowed up.

Moving the paint from the hard surface of the road to the softer, muffling grass covering the benchland, Craig stepped up the pace. He swung wide, not coming at the ranch buildings directly but from well to the south so that he reached a barn with its attached corral before he neared the house itself.

The door to the barn was open and he could see the glow from a lantern spilling faintly into the yard. He tied the paint in a splotch of shadow pressed against the corral fence and eased softly forward toward the light. As he neared the open doorway, he could hear the soft murmur of voices. Loosening the gun in its holster, he stepped to the doorway and turned into the barn itself.

He stopped abruptly, letting his hand fall from his gun.

78

Directly ahead, a lantern hung on a nail driven into a stanchion. Its light fell down into a stall and in the stall was Dwyer, on his knees beside a mare and her newborn foal.

Dwyer said, "That's it, old girl. All done now—and done good too. He's a little beauty. Now up you go. There's a hungry look in the little fellow's eyes. Here . . ."

As if suddenly sensing someone's presence, Dwyer twisted his head toward the doorway. "Marshall What the devil you doing . . . ?" His voice trailed away and a brief flicker of comprehension moved across his face.

Craig said, "Let me give you a hand with the mare." He went into the stall. "That's a real fine colt. I'd say he had a top-grade sire."

"One of Mr. Jerrod's prize stallions," Dwyer said with a touch of pride. "The mare's good too. Look at her legs and her chest when we get her on her feet." He grunted as both men put forth an effort. The mare came up and in less than a minute, the wobbly-legged colt was having its first meal.

Dwyer led the way out of the stall. "I reckon I can leave them for a spell." He got a pitchfork. "As soon as I clean up, you might as well come in. We'll put the coffeepot on and—"

"Thanks just the same," Craig broke in, "but I followed Luvain and two of his men up this way from town."

"Ah," Dwyer murmured, "and when you saw my light, you thought I . . ."

"Let's say I wondered," Craig put in. He realized from Dwyer's expression that the man knew nothing of the night's events and, briefly, he sketched out what had happened.

Dwyer finished changing the straw on the floor of the stall, saw to it that there was food for the mare, and then lifted the lantern from its nail and started out of the barn.

"My guess is that the Luvain bunch is up to no good," he said. "Otherwise Cloyd would have gone home up the valley road. It's the shortest way for him. Least it's the easiest to ride."

Out in the open, he set the lantern down and squatted, picking up a splinter of wood that lay close by. Craig joined him and watched as Dwyer sketched roughly this part of the valley and the hills. "You passed two trails leading kind of northwest as you came up here. Recall them?"

Craig grunted assent. Dwyer went on, "The one nearest here leads into a kind of bowl with a rock wall at the back. The wall sort of bulges out so no one could see a man at the bottom from above. The other day I was following a few head of my ornery stock and I got into the bowl. There was sign of fairly fresh fires there at the back of the bowl and sign that men and horses had been there within the past week—and a number of times before that. A sizable crew of men."

"You're saying that it could be a place where Luvain and his men wait while they're readying for a hit against one of the valley ranches?"

"That or Indians, and I haven't seen one of them since I came to the Sangaree." He shook his head. "No, not Indians. They wouldn't leave the kind of mess I found there."

Craig said thoughtfully, "If it is Luvain and his crew, I wonder what they'd be up to. . . ." He broke off. "That'll be why Jenks was so eager to get Luvain out of jail tonight. They've got a raid set up and need Luvain to lead them!"

"It's a fair guess," Dwyer conceded.

"If there were some way I could get close enough to hear their talk—" Craig began.

Dwyer said quickly, "You can get to the top of the rock wall. It ain't too high, maybe thirty—forty feet. And even if you can't see anybody down below, I figure you could hear them, especially the way voices'll carry on a frosty night like this." He stood up. "Give me five minutes, marshal, and I'll lead you there."

"It's not marshal out here," Craig reminded him. "I'm no more than you or Luvain as far as the law is concerned."

"I never was much for fuss and feathers," Dwyer said. "Nor for titles neither." He started for the house. "If you can saddle me that blaze-faced bay in the barn, it'd save us time." He left the lantern.

Craig took the lantern and went back into the barn, pausing to look over the new mother and her offspring. Both seemed to be doing fine. The mare was tonguing down the colt and getting a lot of sass for her pains. Grinning, Craig moved on until he found the bay. He located Dwyer's saddle on the rack and went to work. When he led the horse into the open, Dwyer was waiting, dressed, a carbine in his hand.

"We can cut right across my front pasture," he said. "We'll be there in jig time."

Craig was glad he had a guide. They angled northwestward across the bench, dipped into a narrow gulch, and climbed up the other side onto a ridge before Dwyer pulled to a halt. He spoke softly now, pointing first to his left where the land broke off roughly, and then on ahead toward the valley stretching out in the darkness.

"The top of the bowl's maybe fifty rods that way," he said. "And from here, there's a kind of trail down the slope to the valley. It's a tight ride but quick if you have to make a run for it."

Leaving the horses, they moved over the rough land on foot, taking the last yards on their bellies. Craig sniffed the chill, quiet air. Well before they reached the top of the rock wall backing the bowl he smelled smoke, and a short time later heard the mutter of voices. At the top of the wall, he lay flat with Dwyer beside him.

The bulge Dwyer had mentioned prevented them from seeing what went on below, but Craig could picture it easily enough. The air carried the smell of boiling coffee well laced with liquor up to them, and it carried voices as well.

Someone said, "Boss, you sure you're ready to ride?"

"We've got an hour yet before the other boys'll be ready," Luvain answered in a thick voice. "I'll be in shape by then. That marshal didn't hit as hard as he thought."

He swore. "The next time I won't play around with him."

There was a strung out silence and then Jenks' voice said, "I still ain't sure what me and my three do, Cloyd. It don't make sense, setting a few little fires when we could burn every haystack in the valley with the coal oil we got here."

"I told you—this isn't the big hit," Luvain snapped. "You do as you're ordered and leave the thinking to me. You and Cram and Lakes and—oh, take Bilks there—you four go straight to Truesdale's hayfield. There's a small rick set off by itself. That's the one you set. Shorty and his crew will hit Finch's place, and I'll lead my outfit to Kearney's. And remember, set the hay and then ride. Don't fool around with stock or the big stacks. Cut right up into the hills and then go to Goldbar on the other side of the ridge. With luck, one of them ranchers'll see some of us riding this way and it'll look for sure like we're heading for Dwyer's. In the dark, they won't know it ain't Dwyer and the other hill men. Is that clear now?"

"It don't make sense," Jenks grumbled, "but it's clear."

It made sense to Craig—too much. With a touch on Dwyer's arm, he wriggled backward to a safe distance and then stood up. Silently the two men made their way back to the horses. Dwyer swore softly. "That's just what'll happen! Luvain starts trouble and Thackaberry and Cardon and me get blamed for it."

"Not tonight," Craig said flatly. "You ride for Thackaberry's place—the quickest way. Roust him out and tell him what's going on. We've got nearly an hour. Maybe we can surprise Luvain a little. You send Thackaberry to Kearney's place and you ride to Finch's. I'll go straight down to the valley and wake Truesdale and tell him what's going to happen. If we move fast enough, Luvain's crews could meet some reception committees."

Dwyer climbed aboard his horse and rode away, wasting no time on words. Craig mounted the paint and started it down the narrow, twisting excuse for a trail that Dwyer had pointed out to him. It was a dangerous ride in the darkness, and once the paint's front hooves rolled on loose rock, but it recovered before Craig lost his seat. Once on the valley floor, Craig put heels to the horse and sent it hammering over the level ground toward the sprawling dark blotch that marked Truesdale's home ranch. He passed great stacks of hay piled up for feed during the long winter. The small rick set off by itself was easy enough to spot and he fixed its location in his mind.

The paint reached the road leading to the ranch and its hooves resounded on the hard ground, the sound carrying clearly on the sharp air. Light showed in the house suddenly as Craig came close. Another light appeared to the left—at the bunkhouse, he guessed.

Then without warning a gun barked sharply and lead whined at him from the right, whipping close to his head. He flattened in the saddle. Another gun opened fire from his left. Craig let out a shout and straightened up, reining in sharply.

A voice cried, "Hold it right there, whoever you are. And let's see you grab for them stars up above. Quick!"

Craig grabbed. "It's Ben Craig," he called. "Get Truesdale down here on the double. Luvain and his outfit are going to fire the hay inside an hour."

More light appeared as the front door to the house swung open, and Craig saw Truesdale coming outside, tucking his nightshirt into the top of his pants. "Craig?"

"That's right."

"Come forward slow and easy."

Craig rode into the light spilling through the door. Truesdale nodded. "All right, men. You heard him. Get saddled up—those of you willing to do a little fighting."

Craig said, "There'll only be four here." Quickly, he told Truesdale what he had heard. "Dwyer's gone for Thackaberry so they can warn Finch and Kearney."

"If they don't get shot trying," Truesdale said dryly. "Both of those two are liable to draw first and think afterward." He slapped cold hands together. "The little rick, you say. I think the boys and I can handle it well enough. You let Martin, my foreman over there, take you to the other ranches. You might get there in time to stop somebody from getting hurt."

A burly man on a solid dun horse rode alongside Craig. They had once had coffee together at Clara's, and now Martin nodded in friendly enough fashion. "Follow me, marshal. There's a quicker way than going back by the road—if you don't mind a little creek water."

Craig loped the paint alongside the dun, going south across the flat valley floor. They moved through hay stubble, crisped from forming frost. At the creek, Martin slowed. "Follow easy. It's got a slippery bottom."

The paint held steady and at this season the water came barely to its knees. On the other side, Martin said, "I saw you whip Luvain tonight, marshal. I figured he'd be in jail at least until Monday."

"Jenks routed out Jerrod and got him to set bail," Craig said shortly. "I wondered what the hurry was. Now I know."

Martin nodded and put spurs to his horse as they hit the level ground again. Finch's place lay only a short distance ahead, and as they neared, lights began to come on. Martin shouted his name loudly, and Finch along with Tip Fraley and three ranchhands were in the yard when Craig and Martin reached it.

A man came riding around the corner of the house. "Someone coming hell bent down the road," he called excitedly.

"That'll be Dwyer," Craig said to Finch. "He was with me tonight when we heard Luvain and his men planning to hit your hay. So listen to what he has to say. We're riding for Kearney's.

"I wouldn't believe a hill man on a stack of—" Finch began.

"Then let your hay burn," Craig snapped. He wheeled the paint around and rode out of the yard, Martin at his heels. Martin drew alongside.

"It'll be all right," he said. "Finch pops off but he'll think now before he shoots—leastwise before he shoots Dwyer."

"If Dwyer got here at the same time we did," Craig worried out loud, "that means Thackaberry will be at Kearney's about now."

As if to punctuate his words, the sound of guns crackling on the sharp air came clearly from the south.

"Thackaberry's arrived," Martin said laconically. Then he swore.

Craig saved his breath and kicked the paint to a dangerous pace over the dark ground.

84

XIV

THEY COULD SEE small blossoms of flame as they neared Kearney's place. The buildings were dark and there was no sign of movement—only the sharp crack of gunfire splitting the night.

"They're coming at us from the north!" someone shouted from near the big barn. A gun cracked and lead whined toward Craig and Martin.

"It's me, Martin, with the marshal!"

"Hold your fire!"

Kearney's deep voice commanded his men to stop shooting. A light came aglow on the porch of the house but no one moved into its range.

"Ride up where we can see you," Kearney ordered.

The two men rode into the glow from the light. Craig swung in the saddle until he located Kearney standing in shadow. "You're a damned fool," he said bluntly. "Do you know who you're shooting at!"

"One of those hill men is my guess," Arty Logan said from Kearney's left.

"Thackaberry," Craig snapped. "And he came here to warn you that Luvain and a crew are going to burn your hay tonight."

"Thackaberry!" Kearney said with heavy contempt. "Does he think I'm fool enough to walk into a trap he'd set?"

Craig cursed him until Kearney came forward, carbine lifted. Craig said, "Lower that gun and listen—for once in your life. I heard Luvain and his outfit planning this. I sent Dwyer to get Thackaberry out of bed and come and warn you. Now what kind of trap do you figure I'm setting for you—Luvain and I together?"

Craig turned the paint. "Thackaberry?" he called. "Are you all right, man?"

Thackaberry's precise lawyer's voice came back from some distance down the road. "If you call lying in a ditch all right, yes. But my horse has been shot. He's dead."

85

Craig said, "You owe Thackaberry one horse, Kearney. And I'd get it for him now if you want his help."

"The devil with his help—and his horse! I'll protect my own hay."

"You've got a lot of it," Craig said. "Which stacks are you going to protect? Thackaberry can tell you. I can tell you. Or you can wait and see which stack goes up in smoke and find out for yourself."

Kearney cursed him heatedly. Craig started the paint east down the road. "Let's go, Martin. They want no help here."

Craig was thirty yards away when Kearney's thick voice stopped him. "All right, Craig. We can have this out later. Arty, go get Thackaberry a horse." He paused and added reluctantly, "One as good as he lost. That satisfy you, Craig?"

"For the time being," Craig said briefly. He told Martin to ride.

He judged the time while he waited. "We've got about fifteen minutes," he said. "How many men can you muster, Kearney?"

"With some of the boys off rounding stuff out of the hills, about six."

"Luvain will only have three with him," Craig said. "He's planning to make a light hit tonight, going after one of your small ricks. He said something about making the big hit later and something about having to wait for some other men to get ready. That could mean an attack from the rear, so I'd leave three of the men to keep guard."

Kearney merely grunted. When Thackaberry rode up, he ignored the man. Thackaberry said, "This horse is better than the one I lost. I'll pay you the difference, Mr. Kearney."

"Go to the devil," Kearney said. He walked to where his horse waited, mounted, and led the way eastward, toward the great piles of hay thrusting up in the darkness.

Counting Craig and Thackaberry, they were six, and when they reached the hay, they spread out, two men each behind two large, nearby stacks, Craig and Thackaberry behind the small rick that was to be the target. There was no sound but the occasional scuffle of a hoof on the frosting grass. After a time, Kearney rode up to Craig.

"Maybe you need your ears looked at, Craig."

"This is the farthest place from where they are meeting," Craig said. "Give it a little more time. They—" He broke off. "Listen!"

The sounds of men riding could be heard plainly now—the clop of hooves, the jangle of harness. There was no effort made to be quiet; the hay was close to the main road and distant from the ranch house. Kearney melted away and Craig risked looking. He could see four riders outlined against the night.

Thackaberry whispered, "If Kearney gets a chance, he'll shoot them out of their saddles with no warning."

"He won't get the chance," Craig said. He rode into the open and lifted his carbine. He sent a bullet screaming out to slash into the ground in front of the lead horse. It reared up, making its rider fight to stay aboard.

"That's far enough, Luvain!" Craig called. "Turn around and get riding."

Kearney's curse rose on the night. His gun bellowed and a man cried out. The four riders broke from their tight knot and fled into the dark, not answering the fire, only riding as hard as they could force their horses. Kearney and his men kept firing, their shots half drowned by Kearney's angry curses.

"You can save your lead," Craig said. "They're out of range." He rode forward toward a dark patch he saw on the ground. Kearney came alongside him.

"What's the matter with you, Craig? I could have got rid of the lot before they knew what hit them."

"Kill them before you knew what they were going to do—the way you tried to kill Thackaberry?"

"You know what they were going to do—burn my hay!"

"Once they started, then you had a right to defend your property. Until then, they had a right to be warned," Craig said.

"Don't give me your town law! There's none of it in this valley."

"Then," Craig said, "if Luvain ever shoots you, don't fig-

87

ure on anyone doing anything about it." He dropped from the saddle and picked up a heavy can. "Coal oil," he said. "There's the proof!"

"It would help at a trial," Craig agreed.

"Then arrest them and we'll have the trial!"

Craig handed him the coal oil can and climbed back in the saddle. A few shots were coming from the north and he started in that direction, Thackaberry at his side. He called back, "Out here, Kearney, I can't arrest anybody. You said as much yourself." He kicked the pace of the paint up to a ground-swallowing lope.

The shooting was over quickly and by the time Craig and Thackaberry reached Finch's place, the trouble seemed finished for the night. Truesdale had ridden down and now a large group of men milled in the warmth of Finch's big parlor, drinking coffee prepared by his sleepy-eyed cook.

"I gave 'em a couple of warning shots," Finch explained to Craig, "and told 'em to get riding. One got a little feisty and shot back, but Dwyer here nicked his horse across the rump and the four took off like scalded heifers."

"We ran our bunch off easy enough too," Truesdale agreed. "I—" He broke off as the front door slammed open and Kearney came lurching into the room. His heavy features were twisted with anger.

"Thirty!" he cried. "Those thirty head of prime breeding stock I was special feeding. They're gone!"

Craig felt the jolt of understanding take him in the belly. Now he understood what Luvain had meant about having to wait an hour for the other boys to be ready. While everyone was occupied near the hay, it had been an easy enough matter for a crew to slip in and make off with what everyone knew was Kearney's great pride.

"The night man got roped right out of his saddle and then slammed on the head with a gun butt. By the time he came around, the stock was gone." He swung his massive head as if seeking a scapegoat. "He didn't even know how many there were."

Finch motioned to his foreman. "Tip, you'd better go check on those ten specials we put in that field on the west side."

88

"I've got a dozen myself that need looking after," Truesdale remarked, but Martin was already on his way.

Kearney continued to glare around, and now his eyes lingered longest on Thackaberry and Dwyer, both of whom were standing close to Craig. "He's trying to twist what happened into being our fault," Thackaberry muttered softly to Craig.

Kearney strode toward the little group, his finger stabbing. "Come daylight, I'm taking a crew into the hills. And by God if I find any of my prize stock on your land—either of yours—you'd better start packing, because by sundown I'm going to burn you out!"

"It's a good thing we didn't help him more," Dwyer said in a thin voice, "or he'd shoot us down right here."

Kearney swelled up as he sucked in a deep, angry breath. Before he could speak, Thackaberry said mildly, "I can see his reasoning. When Craig showed up unexpectedly at your place, Dwyer, you had to think fast to keep him from finding out our connection with Luvain. So you took him where he could overhear the plans, knowing full well that the hay burning was only a decoy and that the true targets were the prize stock over in the west pastures. Then when you rode to warn me, of course you first stopped and told Luvain what had happened. That's why his crews rode off with so little fuss. All they wanted to do anyway was create a diversion. Naturally, Mr. Kearney figured this all out with no trouble."

Everyone but Kearney caught the sarcasm in Thackaberry's brief speech. Kearney cried, "So you admit it!" Truesdale burst out laughing, and even Finch joined in. Kearney, red-faced, turned to glare around him. "Be careful, Thackaberry," Craig said. "You make out too good a case for the other side. Kearney might use your words against you in court—he obviously believes them."

"And as obviously, he'll never believe otherwise," Thackaberry said. "Mr. Kearney is a perfect example of the man who cannot separate his beliefs and prejudices from fact—no matter how different they're proved to be. To his mind, what he thinks is truth—always and forever."

Kearney's flush grew heavier. "What's all that lawyer talk supposed to mean?" he demanded roughly.

"That when you get an idea fixed in your head, nothing on earth is going to change it," Craig said quietly. "In other words, you're blind and bullheaded and so satisfied with your own opinion of yourself, that you'll let yourself be ruined before you'd as much as admit—even deep inside—that you could be wrong."

"I'll whip you for that!" Kearney cried. He took a step forward.

Finch intervened, catching him by the arms. "Calm down," he snapped. "Thackaberry and Craig are right, and you know it. The hill men had no more to do with taking our stock than Craig himself. I'm beginning to agree with Truesdale and doubt if they ever did."

"Maybe Craig did have a hand in it!" Kearney shouted. He was still obviously wild from the loss of his prize herd. "If he didn't, why ain't he out looking for my stock? Why did he drive Luvain off with a warning instead of shooting him out of the saddle? He's done a lot of talking about coming here to kill Luvain, but every chance he gets, he backs off."

"I told you why I drove Luvain off," Craig said reasonably. "As for my hunting down your stock, why should I? I'm not your hired hand, Kearney. But if it turns up inside the town limits, I'll let you know."

Truesdale said, "I suggest we take another vote on whether or not Craig should be the law in the whole Sangaree. We know how Cardon and Jerrod feel; the rest of the property owners are here so it should be legal enough."

"You trying to whipsaw me into changing my vote?" Kearney demanded.

"I'm just trying to get you to use your head to think with instead of using it only to bellow with," Truesdale said bluntly. "You keep telling Craig to act like the law but you don't want to give him the power. You can't have it both ways."

Kearney rubbed a rough hand across his jaw. "I ain't sure—oh, hell, what have I got to lose?"

"Some tax money to help pay for the extra protection you get," Craig said dryly. He added, "If I decide to take on that much work."

Kearney opened his mouth again but Dwyer managed to

speak up first. "We'd all sure appreciate it, marshal. The way it is, we got to watch our stock and try to make a living and keep an eye on each other all at the same time. Maybe you could wipe out all the suspicion and trouble if you were the law in these parts."

Kearney thrust his jaw forward belligerently. "And what if you find the stock on these hill squatters' land?"

Craig said, "I'll take the same steps as if I found their stock in one of your pastures."

Truesdale's appreciative chuckle was stopped by Martin and Tip Fraley. They came hurrying into the room, their expressions telling plainly enough what had happened. "They got our special herds too," Fraley said. He shook his head. "Over fifty head of top-grade beef gone in one night!"

"That's a pretty fair-sized herd to push very far very fast," Craig said. He glanced through the window to his left. The first hint of dawn showed over the eastern ridge. "My guess is that they'll try to run the stock into some gully somewhere and hold it during the day and then push it on over the border tonight." He shook his head. "But I don't know this country well enough to even guess where you could hide fifty-odd head safely."

"Luvain's crew couldn't get the stock to Goldbar much before noon," Finch agreed. "I'd say they probably choused the herd into the west side mountains. There are plenty of dead-end gulches to run them into."

"If we're so sure it's one of Luvain's crews that took our beef, then I say let's go to Goldbar and clean out the lot of them!" Kearney cried.

"We aren't sure," Craig said. "Not sure enough to start a war about it—not yet. And if we do get proof, then is the time to get up a posse and go after them."

"And take them to town for a trial, I suppose," Kearney said heavily.

"If I'm the law here, that's the way it'll be," Craig said. He met Kearney's angry gaze. "Besides, man, what do you think would happen if every man here willing to fight rode to Goldbar today? Luvain and his hardcases wouldn't just send a few warning shots—they'd cut us down, every man of us."

"Then what do you want to do?" Kearney demanded.

Craig looked around. "Who knows the west side hills— say from a point opposite Truesdale's place on north to the border? Who knows them best?"

"I do," Truesdale admitted. "I ran a lot of cattle in there until Cardon took the land. And I'd say he's pretty familiar with the area too."

"All right," Craig said, "then let's you and Cardon and I and three other men go cow hunting. Starting now."

"Count me in," Kearney said.

"I'd rather have Arty Logan," Craig answered. "He doesn't have as itchy a trigger finger." He glanced around. "How about you, Tip? You should know that country."

"Tip can go," Finch said.

"I've helped Cardon a lot," Dwyer said. "I'll join in."

Kearney was still angry, but he said, "All right, take Arty. And you, Craig, just watch out that those hill men don't cross you up and start signaling Luvain's outfit."

"He'll never learn," Thackaberry remarked. With a nod to Finch for the coffee, he walked out. In a few minutes, Kearney stalked away as well, muttering something about sending Logan over.

Finch shook his head. "And I thought I was a stubborn Irisher!" He shouted for the cook. "We'd better put something under your belts, gents, before you head into the hills. It could be a long day."

It could indeed, Craig agreed silently. And one that might not see them all come back.

XV

ONE OF Finch's men rode for Cardon, and he arrived just as the group was finishing breakfast. He listened in his quiet, serious way, and then said, "I can make a pretty good guess where we'll find them."

Out in the yard, he squatted down and with a twig made a rough sketch of the west mountains. "Up here is a canyon," he said. "It looks like a dead end but there's a narrow twisting gut that breaks into another canyon. That one angles

92

this way—pretty much north—and goes all the way across the border." He drew another line. "This is the trail up from Goldbar. You can push stock from there up past the mines and into any of these high country box draws." His twig moved a few more times, outlining the draws. "And this trail branches off the one going to Goldbar and hooks into the canyon."

He squinted up at the sky. "If the cattle were taken about midnight, they're probably close to being pushed through the gut right now. If Luvain's men can keep them moving, and if it doesn't make up a storm out of the north, they can have them across the border by tonight."

"With that kind of passage into Canada, they don't need to hole up all day," Craig agreed. "Is there any way we can cut over and drop into the big canyon without going through Goldbar? If we could get ahead of the drive instead of having to trail it all the way, we'd stand a good chance of stopping it."

"I know the canyon he's talking about," Tip Fraley said. "And there's a mean trail that cuts over a pass about three miles this side of Goldbar that'll drop us right down in it."

"That's right," Cardon agreed. "The trail comes in just before the canyon starts climbing into the snow country. It gets pretty steep the last few miles before the border."

Craig straightened up. "Check your guns, gents, and consider yourself deputized. Now let's ride."

Arty Logan arrived as they were leaving the yard. Bunched, the six rode into spreading morning light. With fresh horses under them, they made good time across the flat valley. This was Craig's first time so far north and he watched with interest as the mountains began to squeeze in until there was little left ahead but a canyon for the river to run through. After a time, he could make out the small smudge on the canyon's side, marking Goldbar, but before they drew close enough for anything to stand out plainly, Cardon reined abruptly to his left and up a short, steep slope of barely marked trail.

At the top of the steep stretch, a flat ran straight westward for a short distance and then the trail began to twist down and up, from gulch to rimrock and back. Craig began

93

to feel the change in the air as they climbed, and when Cardon finally stopped to let the horses blow, there was the taste of snow on the thin wind whistling down from the north.

Cardon pointed toward a rough edge of rimrock ahead. "The trail goes over that down to the bottom of the canyon."

"How far?" Craig wanted to know.

"Some two hundred feet," Cardon said. He added dryly, "Straight down, that is. I'd guess maybe a half mile by trail."

Craig glanced back to see the sun beginning its climb. "Let's move on," he said.

They moved, Cardon still leading the way. It was a touchy trail, Craig discovered—in most places little more than narrow natural ledges hanging from the sheer rock wall of the canyon and the ledges joined by tracks chopped from the living stone by some enterprising prospector to give footing for his burro. At least, Craig thought, they were out of the icy wind here. Given any kind of weather, this excuse for a trail would be impassable.

Six men breathed sighs of open relief as their horses planted their hooves on the solid, rocky bottom of the canyon. Craig glanced around at sheer walls rising easily two hundred feet up. Behind them, to the north, the canyon bottom began a steep climb. Ahead, it was level, at least to the shoulder of rock that lay some twenty-odd yards farther along.

Cardon trotted his horse forward a short distance and then came back. "No fresh sign in that sandy spot ahead," he said in his laconic way. "They haven't got this far yet."

Craig pointed to the shoulder of rock. "What's the lay of the canyon below that?"

"It slopes down a little," Cardon said. "But it's wide and flat, with no cover—if that's what you were wondering."

Craig nodded. "Then the best we can do is pull up behind the shoulder there. When the point man comes, I suggest we rope him and try to keep him quiet. We don't know how many there'll be, but anyone not riding point will have to stay behind the herd. There isn't room between the far wall and the edge of the shoulder for more than four head of stock at a time, let alone a flank rider."

They lined their horses along the side of the outcropping

94

of rock. Truesdale unlimbered his rope. "This is my pleasure," he said. "I'm not much with a gun, but I can loop a gnat at fifty paces."

Craig motioned him to the front of the line. "Let's get out a few more ropes," he ordered. "There could be more than one man at point."

He started to say more but stopped as the sound of cattle bellowing came clearly to them up the canyon. Then they heard the rough shouts of men urging the animals on. Cardon listened intently. He said, "From the echoes I'd say another five minutes."

Craig loosened his carbine and motioned for the others to do the same. The sounds grew louder as the minutes ticked away. A man's voice came clearly, close enough to make Arty Logan start a little.

"All right, you two on the flanks, drop back. I'll point the way. Keep them bunched tight until they're all past this rock."

"Only one at point," Craig breathed softly to Truesdale.

The rancher nodded and readied his rope. The ground was rough here and the sounds of a horse's hooves rolling small rocks came sharp and clear. A man appeared abruptly, lean, needing a shave, battered gear and worn clothing testifying to the tightrope existence he lived.

Truesdale let him get well past the rock and then threw his loop. It arced out perfectly and settled over his shoulders. A grunt of surprise was all he could manage before he was jerked from the saddle and slammed to the gound, the wind gushing out of him. As soon as he hit, Tip Fraley was there. His .44 rose and fell, the butt biting through the man's hat. He jerked once and lay still. At the same time, Craig sent his horse out and gathered in the reins of the point man's mount. He brought the horse back quickly.

Cardon still had his head cocked. "Nothing," he said. "They didn't see a thing."

The first of the herd was coming now. Craig counted them off to himself as they moved past the rock three and four abreast. When fifty had passed, he lifted a hand. A man shouted and one lone cow galloped awkwardly to join the others. The first pair of riders appeared, pushing their horses as the cattle had got a little ahead of them. They rode straight, not looking to the side, their attention fixed on the stock and on regaining their flank positions.

The taller one groaned. "Look at that slope. I need a rest before I tackle that."

"The boss said get 'em over the border first," the second man answered. He turned in the saddle. "Come on you two. Hustle—" He broke off as he saw the six men lined up, saw the six carbines leveled at him. His hands flew high, jerking the reins and stopping his horse.

"Bones," he croaked faintly.

The other man turned and now his hands reached for the slit of sky showing above the canyon rim. From just below the shoulder of rock, a voice shouted, "What's going on up there?"

Then the final pair appeared, men cut in the same ragged mold as the others. The heavier of the pair made a move toward his gun when he saw Craig and his group but a snap shot from Craig's carbine whipped past his hat and he changed his mind.

"Just keep reaching, all four of you," Craig said.

"Who the devil are you?" the man called Bones demanded.

"I own some of those cows," Truesdale said quietly. He nodded toward Arty Logan and Tip Fraley, who were spurring ahead now to stop the herd before it could start up the slope. "Those two represent the owners of the rest of the beef. And this gent is the law in these parts. The rest of us are deputies."

"Law! They told us there wasn't any law in the Sangaree!" Bones protested.

"There is now," Craig said. "So get moving. You boys have got a nice warm jail to sleep in tonight."

The heavy-set man kicked spurs into his horse and sent it ramming forward. Craig snapped another shot at him and missed. Then the man was weaving through the herd. Arty Logan drew his gun and let it drop—to shoot and miss would mean risking hitting the men bunched below. The rider kept going, flat in the saddle, kicking his horse viciously. Tip Fraley took a shot at him as he went past, and swore as his bullet bounded off the canyon wall. Then the man was around a bend and out of sight.

"He'll ride to Goldbar and warn Luvain," Truesdale said.

"In that case," Craig said, "we'd better get these cattle back where they belong as quick as we can."

They tied the four remaining men in their saddles, the unconscious one belly-down, and started back down the trail. When the sun was noon high, they were back in the valley. If Luvain knew of the loss of the cattle, he hadn't seen fit to take any action, Craig thought. He sagged in the saddle with weariness.

They dropped Truesdale's part of the herd off in his feed lot and then pushed the remainder on toward Finch's place. Tip Fraley rode alongside Craig. "Now that you're the law here, marshal, what do you plan to do about Luvain and that hog wallow up at Goldbar?"

"Why," Craig said, "I figured on paying the place a visit—as soon as I get a little sleep and some food under my belt. If it's a hog wallow, like you say, then I guess I'll be going on a boar hunt."

Luvain came into town in heavy darkness, making a wide swing away from the road so that he crossed the river by the darkened sawmill. He left his horse and moved through shadow around the hotel stable and into a small side door. He drifted down a hallway and carefully, moving only when he was sure not to be seen, made his way to Jerrod's fancy suite on the second floor. His quick rap brought footsteps. Jerrod opened the door, grimaced when he saw the still swollen face, and motioned Luvain inside.

"All hell's broke loose," Luvain said. He went to a sideboard and poured himself a drink from a bottle standing there. He gulped down the liquor. "One of those drifters I hired to take them cows got lucky. The rest were caught by Craig and a whole crew. The drifter told me Craig claims to be the law in the valley now."

"He came in this afternoon," Jerrod said. "And the drifter is right." He smiled. "What are you worrying about? That's just what we wanted, isn't it? What does it matter if a few scum are in jail?"

Luvain gulped down a second drink and then dropped heavily into a chair. He began to shape a cigarette. "The ramrod of the scum, as you call 'em, happens to be one Craig caught. And he knows more'n he should. I don't trust Bones or any of his outfit. They could start blabbing, hoping to save their own hides."

Jerrod's gaze was sharp. "Just how much does this Bones know?"

"He knows that I set the whole shebang up, doesn't he? I hired him." He stopped, licking his cigarette slowly.

"How much more does he know?" Jerrod demanded in a deadly soft tone.

"If you mean does he know about you—not exactly," Luvain said. He took time to light his cigarette. "But I told him that if he and his boys did a good job last night, there might be more work for them—like helping us make a real big hit. I made mention that all we were waiting for was word from the big boss."

"You crazy fools!"

"He ain't got no name to throw around," Luvain said.

"Even so, if he talks, Craig will be warned. You know what he'll do with the authority he has. He'll round up a posse of town men and another one of valley and hill men and stop anything you start!"

"I been thinking that," Luvain admitted. "And from the descriptions of the ones with Craig I got out of that drifter, it sounds like the valley ranchers and the hill ones made their peace."

"Thanks to your trick last night," Jerrod agreed.

"Even so," Luvain pursued, "without Craig, the people around here ain't much. Excepting you, who else is there to lead 'em?"

"Nobody," Jerrod acknowledged. "So what do you intend to do—gun Craig down?" His voice thickened. "Or fist fight him again?"

"All right, so he can whip me and he can outdraw me. I still got a way figured out to take care of him."

Jerrod went to the sideboard and poured himself a drink. He sipped at it. "I'm listening."

"We make the big hit just the way we planned—burn all

the valley hay, run off all the stock we can, leave them three puffed toads with nothing but their shirts to get through the winter on. Then you can buy them up the way you figured—and we'll own the valley."

"I told you, Craig will stop you. He's that kind." Jerrod grimaced. "I really caught a bear by the tail when I decided to use him."

"Craig won't be around." Luvain grinned. "You'll have to take over and get the posse shaped up. Now if I should happen to let someone like Dwyer overhear some of my plans and he should come running to you with his mouth flapping, you might just lead that posse to the wrong place."

Jerrod thrust out his lower lip in thought. "It just might work. With Craig out of the way, we could make it work."

"You leave Craig to me," Luvain said.

"Just how . . . ?"

Luvain interrupted him. "Let me take care of it." His lips stretched in a thin smile. "Craig's got a weak spot. I figured out what it is—and that's where I'm going to hit him. Tomorrow he'll ride out of Sangaree, hell bent."

He got to his feet. "I got work to do and I suspect you'll want to be getting on home."

"I'm staying here tonight," Jerrod said. "Now let's hear your plan."

Luvain gave no sign that Jerrod's staying in the hotel pleased him. He said, "The less you or anybody else knows, the better you'll like it." He moved toward the door. "Only keep this in mind, Jerrod. When Craig rides out of town tomorrow, he ain't never coming back—not alive, he ain't."

He opened the door and slipped out into the hall. The door shut behind him with an almost deadly quiet.

XVI

LUVAIN STOOD in shadow by the window of the sunroom. Anita was a faint blur of light against the darkness that squeezed down on Jerrod's house.

"Why must you fight?" she whispered. "I heard about what happened, what Craig did to you."

"There's no time for that," Luvain said. "We're in trouble."

A gasp ran out of her. "Someone knows—about us?"

"Craig knows," he said. He sounded unconcerned. "But that isn't the trouble I'm talking about. I'm in trouble and so is your husband."

She sounded frightened. "Cloyd, I don't understand."

His voice was low and quick. "Listen carefully. I ain't got much time. I came here to get your help—for me and Jerrod."

He moved slightly forward, bringing himself a bit closer to her. "Craig's got to be taken care of. That's a job I'm going to enjoy, but it won't be easy. I can't come to town after him—he's got too many friends. The same thing's true in the valley since he made himself the law out there. So I've got to get him up in the hills where we can have it out with nobody to interfere."

"Cloyd, you can't face down Craig. He—he'll kill you."

"He won't get the chance," Luvain said flatly. "That ain't the part that worries me—killing him. But getting him into the hills, that's the problem. And that's where you help."

"But I hardly know the man," she protested. "I've spoken to him a few times but that's all."

"You know his woman," Luvain said. "I been figuring and from all I hear she's his only weakness. My guess is that if Marnie Clayton is taken into the hills and Craig hears about it, he'll go after her. And when he does, I'll be waiting."

"Cloyd, you're going to—to take the girl? You're going to kill her?" The horror in her voice raised it to a shrill pitch.

"Be quiet!" he snapped. "And don't be a fool, Anita. I ain't got nothing against her. As soon as she's done her part of the job—getting Craig into the hills—she'll be packed back home."

"But what will you gain by doing all this? Why, Cloyd?"

"I'll gain half the Sangaree valley and half the town, that's what," he said. "Me and Jerrod—we'll be partners." He laughed softly. "And then, maybe, Jerrod won't be around and I'll have it all—for you and me together."

"Cloyd, what's come over you? I know you've had to fight for your existence, fight against your background—but you've never been like this before. So ruthless!"

"This is my chance to get rich," he said. "This is my chance to be a big man, to own things like other people. To have all the money I want, the best food and the best liquor. And to have the prettiest woman in the world. All to myself. To get all that, I'll do what I have to do."

She took a deep steadying breath. "I won't help you, Cloyd. Not this time. I won't help you murder. I'm no fool. I know what you intend to do after you kill Craig. You'll raid the valley and ruin the men there. There'll be more killing, more destruction. I won't help. I can't!"

So mildly that he seemed to have been expecting her attitude, Luvain said. "In that case, you better figure on being poor again—the way you was when Jerrod found you. Because if I don't ruin the valley ranchers, all the money Jerrod has laid out trying to get their land—everything he owns—will be lost." He thrust his face toward her. "Or didn't you know your husband's been taking money from his bank to pay me and my boys—other people's money?"

"No!"

"That's the way it is," Luvain said flatly. "It's too late for Jerrod to back out now. The way I go, he goes. If I win, he wins. If I lose, he loses. And if he loses, so do you. Everything you've got here."

She was silent for some time before saying, "I have to think it over."

"There ain't no time for that. I want Craig tomorrow. Because tomorrow night—at midnight—we're going to hit the valley. That means Craig's woman has got to be taken about the time it first gets dark. I got to know now what you'll do."

Silence again. And then her voice, dull, hopeless: "Tell me what I have to do, Cloyd."

He moved even closer and spoke quickly, outlining his plan. Finished, he said, "See, it ain't so much. All you've got to do is get the message to Craig—I don't care how—that you saw Marnie Clayton being taken and you recognized one of the men. Say it was one you saw up at the pass that day Craig shot Pete. That's all."

"When?"

"If you decided to go to the hotel for dinner, you'd get there about six. By then, she'll be gone. So right after six o'clock. That's when you get the message to Craig."

"All right," she said. She sounded listless. Luvain reached up and drew her toward him, but she turned her head aside. "I don't want you to kiss me, Cloyd. Not now. Not until your face heals."

"That gives me one more good reason for killing Craig," he said.

Anita Jerrod remained at the window until his footsteps had faded from her hearing. Then she went slowly to bed. She lay awake a long time. When she finally fell asleep it was to dream and waken trembling and frightened. In the darkness, she suddenly found herself seeing Cloyd Luvain as he really was. And then the thought came to her that he might be lying about her husband. She resolved to ask Park in the morning.

She fell soundly asleep at last, wondering how strong her resolve would be in daylight.

Day came cold and sullen. The taste of snow was in the air, its threat in the flat, low clouds that pressed down on the valley, cutting off the upper halves of the mountains. Anita Jerrod slept late, exhausted from her nearly sleepless night. She ate little, finding food tasteless, her one interest the return of her husband so that she could talk to him.

By early afternoon Jerrod had not returned home and finally Anita dressed, had her buggy brought, and rode through the growing chill to town. She saw Craig going into the marshal's office as she ran the buggy up to the hotel and for a moment she was tempted to go to him, tell him what she had learned. But until she knew the truth, she could not. She had to give Park a chance to defend himself against Cloyd's accusations. After she talked to Park, if what Cloyd had said was true, then she could go to Craig.

As she left the buggy, the first thin spits of snow came

102

down, almost like frozen mist, stinging her face. Drawing her coat up against the side of her face, she hurried into the lobby and started for the stairs. The clerk's soft call stopped her. "If you're looking for Mr. Jerrod, Mrs. Jerrod, he's gone out on business."

"To the ranch?"

"No, ma'am, to see Dwyer, he told me. He left an hour or so ago."

Thanking him with a nod, Anita hurried back to the buggy. She thought again of going to Craig but for the same reason as before pushed the desire away. Hurrying home, she changed to her riding clothes and had her blaze-faced sorrel mare brought around. One of her few pleasures was riding and she had explored as much of these eastern hills as she could manage on horseback.

Now she made no effort to ride down to the valley and follow the road there; instead she took the narrow and, in places, treacherous ridge trail. But where Luvain had turned to drop through the dry wash to the valley road, she kept on, winding her way over bare tracks, dipping into gulches and climbing onto ridges—following a route she had taken many times just for the sheer pleasure of being this high up, this far away from people.

But today she was not riding for pleasure. The spits of snow she had felt in town were swirling here on the ridges and she pushed the sorrel as fast as she dared. As a result, she reached the hills behind Dwyer's place within half the time she would have taken by the valley road.

She dropped down to Dwyer's yard and found him stacking firewood against the impending storm. His surprise when she rode up was evident. She said, "Oh, my husband's gone already?"

"Mr. Jerrod? He hasn't been here," Dwyer said.

She started to say, "But I was told—" and checked herself. Instead, she said, "Oh, I heard he was in the valley on business and I just supposed he'd come here."

"I'm sorry, Mrs. Jerrod, but I haven't seen him." He rose from his work. "You must be cold from that ride. If you'll come in, I'm sure my wife has a pot of coffee on the back of the stove."

103

Anita smiled her thanks with facial muscles that were stiffer from cold than she had realized. But she shook her head. "I think I'll get back before the storm really comes. It won't be so bad with the wind against me." She started away and then reined the sorrel in. Turning, she said as casually as she could, "I know this sounds silly but ever since I heard of the way you and the marshal found out what the Luvain gang was planning to do to the ranchers, I've wanted to have a look at their meeting place. Is it close to here?"

Dwyer grinned the way a man will at what he regards as a woman's foolishness. "It's a gully on the way to the valley and a little north." Picking up a piece of kindling, he sketched the location of the gully for her. "But I wouldn't do more than take a quick look, Mrs. Jerrod. That storm looks to be making for certain."

"I may not even stop," she said. "But I am curious." With a smile of goodbye, she cantered the sorrel around his house and down the lane toward the valley. Once she had seen Dwyer's sketch, the particular gully was clear in her mind—she had taken refuge from a summer rain there once, she remembered. But this time she rode as Craig and Dwyer had, to the rimrock rather than into the gully itself. And as they had done, she left the horse and walked to the edge of the gully.

She was hoping against hope that the hunch that had brought her here would prove to be nothing. But she could hear the soft murmur of voices before she reached the rimrock itself, and soon she could smell campfire smoke. At the rim she paused and lay flat. The heavy air and the hiss of fine snow on the thin wind floated much of the sound away from her but she was able to recognize Cloyd Luvain's bayou drawl and the crisp, commanding tones of her husband easily. She heard, "Even if the storm lets up, that hay'll be pretty wet." That was Cloyd, she thought.

Jerrod said, "Then take a lot of coal oil. It has to be tonight, storm or no storm. For what you and your men will get out of this, you should be able to stand a little snow and cold."

A rise in the wind wafted the remainder of their words

away. But she had heard enough. Rising, she made her way quickly back to the sorrel and climbed into the saddle. She looked through the misting snow to the valley, hazy below. No, she dared not go that way. She might run into Cloyd going north or Park going south. She would have to go back the way she had come. It would be quicker if the trails weren't too badly snow-covered.

Her whole concentration was fixed on taking the tiring little horse over the narrow, dangerous trail, and it was not until she had it back in its stall, the handyman unsaddling it, that she realized how late it had become. With the storm darkness had begun to fall early. Even so, she thought, it must be close to five o'clock.

And now the full meaning of what she had overheard struck her. She could no longer deny any possibility of Park's part in this scheme—in what amounted to the capture of Marnie Clayton and the killing of Craig—let alone what would happen to the valley ranchers and their years of labor.

"Harness the trotter to the buggy," she directed the handyman. She waited nervously until he was finished and then she climbed into the buggy and started for town. Coming out of the warmth of the stable, she was surprised to find how dark it had become and how much thicker the snow was. No longer a fine mist, it had turned into sharp-edged flakes blown on a rising wind. She had to fight the horse to keep it from turning against the icy gusts, and it took all of her strength to swing north around the bank and force the horse as far as the jail building.

Quickly she swung the buggy around so that the shivering animal faced south. Tying it, she hurried into the log building and into the warmth of the jail office. She ignored the rude sounds made by the four men in the cells. Craig was not there, but Briggs was.

He got to his feet. "Mrs. Jerrod?"

"I'm looking for the marshal," she said. "It's very important."

"I'm sorry," Briggs said, "but Arty Logan came in and took him out to the valley—to Finch's place, I think—for a meeting. There's a rumor that Luvain and his outfit are going to make their big hit soon and the ranchers wanted the marshal to do some planning—now that he's their law too."

She said quickly, "That's what I wanted to tell him. I heard that the attack is going to be tonight."

"You're sure? How do you . . ." But she was gone, leaving Briggs gaping at the empty doorway.

Anita climbed into the buggy and sent the horse sliding and slithering down the now slippery street toward the lights of Clara's café. If she couldn't warn Craig, at least she could warn Marnie and Clara. At the café, she hurried out of the buggy and into the small room. It was empty and there was no odor of cooking, despite the clock on the wall reading five forty-five.

"Miss Clayton?" she called. Then in a louder voice: "Clara?" The sound came again. She opened the door to the storage pantry, letting light from the kitchen fall into the darkness of the tiny room. Anita gasped. Clara lay on the floor, contorted by ropes binding her ankles and arms, a gag pushed crudely into her mouth.

Anita found a knife and quickly cut Clara free. With the gag out, Clara found breath enough to cry, "Marnie! They took Marnie."

"When?" Anita demanded.

"Fifteen or twenty minutes ago. Help me, please. I have to see the marshal and tell him. It was Luvain's crew, I'm sure. I recognized the one they call Jenks."

So Cloyd didn't trust her, Anita thought. He had said six o'clock, but his men had taken Marnie over a half hour before that time. And just in case, Jenks had let himself be recognized by Clara so that, once free, she would have been able to identify him as one of the men who had taken Marnie away.

And suddenly, irrationally, she found herself not just unsure of her feelings for Cloyd Luvain, but hating him violently.

She said, "The marshal is at Finch's place. We can get riding horses at the hotel. Hurry!"

XVII

CRAIG WAS SAYING, "Don't be too sure Luvain won't hit you just because of a storm. He might like—" and then he stopped as the front door to Finch's big parlor was flung open, letting in a howl of wind, a spate of snow, and two snow-caked women.

Clara pushed the door shut and stood panting. "Marnie," she gasped. "Luvain's men have taken Marnie away."

A babble of voices arose, questioning, demanding, and then Anita Jerrod shrugged out of her snow-covered greatcoat and her soft voice cut through the rumble of noise, silencing the men. She said, "It's a plan to get the marshal away from here—to trap him and kill him. Tonight. Then the attack will come and—"

Craig stepped forward. "How do you know, Mrs. Jerrod? Who told you?"

He saw the truth in her expression and he understood her moment of silence. When she said, "I happened to overhear Cloyd Luvain and some of his men talking," he made no effort to contradict her. She went on, explaining that she had felt like a ride and had suddenly found herself facing a storm. So she turned for Dwyer's place and then decided to try to get home instead of staying there.

"Out of curiosity I asked him about the place where he and Mr. Craig had overheard those—those men talking. He told me where it was and I stopped there on my way into the valley. I heard them talking—about taking Marnie Clayton and—and everything I've said. For heaven's sake, don't stand here. Do something!"

It was a rather weak explanation, Craig thought, but the men were too excited to think about it. He said, "All right, I suggest you start posting your men. They're bound to try to fire your hay and maybe even try to burn your barns." He swung on Clara. "Can you get back to town and tell Briggs to form a posse, to get all the townsmen he can? We'll need all the help we can get out here. We don't know how many hardcases Luvain has rounded up for this attack and we don't know when it's coming."

"Not until midnight," Anita said. "I heard Cloyd—Luvain say that before the attack, he wanted to be sure you were dead."

"That means he was counting on Craig here going after Marnie," Truesdale said.

"And he's right," Craig snapped. "You all have guns and you know how to use them. Briggs can lead the towns-men here as easily as I could. You don't need me."

"We wouldn't get you if we did," Truesdale observed, but he smiled faintly as he said it.

Kearney lumbered toward the door, shrugging into his coat. "By midnight, we'll have a little surprise waiting over at my spread." He went on out. Truesdale followed and in a moment Finch left, calling loudly for Tip Fraley.

Craig turned to Clara. "Get moving. It'll take all the time we have to spare to get the townsmen here."

"I'm going with you to find Marnie." Her voice was flat, empty.

"No," Anita said. "You can't. She's being taken into the hills up toward the border—behind the mines. And it's a trap. You'll be killed."

"Believe me," Craig said earnestly, "I can handle it better alone, Clara. You take Mrs. Jerrod and get back to town. I'm counting on you to make up the posse. You can argue the men into it better than Briggs can."

He saw Clara staring at Anita Jerrod. "How does she know so much about it?" Clara demanded.

"There's no time for that now," Craig said. He turned to Anita. "Explain to her later. Right now, I want to know everything that might help me find Marnie!"

She spoke in a low, steady voice. "Cloyd told me that he intends to take Marnie up the big canyon that leads to the border. He said he was going to make sure that there was enough sign for you to follow easily. About halfway up the steep part, where the canyon climbs toward the border, there's a side canyon. He's going to be waiting there, way back in and—Marnie will be near the front where you can see her. When you ride to get her, he's going to kill you."

"He told you to tell me all this?"

"No, but I think he suspected I might." She explained

108

about how she had been tricked on the time. "He didn't trust me, I know now."

"If that's the case," Craig said, "he'll have his trap set someplace else." He reached for his greatcoat and worked into it. He drew his .44 and checked it carefully. "Thank you, Mrs. Jerrod—whatever happens. And now you both get riding. It'll be easier with the wind at your back but don't take any risks. The ranchers need the townsmen desperately."

He left them, using a moment to feel pity for Anita Jerrod, faced with explaining herself to Clara Clayton and hoping that Clara would be tolerant enough to forgive even though she might not understand. Then he was fighting the wind to reach the barn where the paint waited.

Finch was there, talking to his men, He said in a thick voice, "Marshal, I can spare a man or two if you need . . ."

"Thanks anyway," Craig interrupted. "But this is better handled alone." He checked his cinch and then mounted the horse. "Use your extra men to get the hill ranchers down here. Maybe then, when it's over Kearney will be completely convinced whose side they're on." Swinging the paint around, he headed it out into the biting night.

The wind had begun drifting the snow and Craig had to ride slowly at first to keep the paint on the easiest path. It would have a lot of riding to do tonight, he knew. Then he became aware of a strange stillness and as he lifted his head there was no feel of snow stinging his face, no feel of icy wind cutting at him.

Ahead he could see a night sky sharp with cold, hard stars. He glanced behind. The trailing edge of the clouds that had carried the storm was well down the valley, pushing snow and wind before it, and leaving deadly, cold silence behind.

Without the wind in the paint's face, the sturdy animal made better time. Craig followed the route he had taken with Dwyer and the others. He refused to let his mind dwell on Marnie; that only meant wild, shaking anger against Luvain, anger that blotted out any chance he had of thinking clearly. Instead he tried to guess what Luvain would do—and basing his guess on five long years of tracking the man, he thought he knew.

109

Where the trail branched from the valley over the hills to the canyon, Craig paused, wondering if his guess was right. He shook his head. He had no guideposts but his own judgment, his own knowledge of the man. If he changed his plan now because of indecision, he might change it again and again—and gain nothing. Resolutely, he kept the paint heading up the valley for Goldbar.

The few lights marking the place grew brighter and then Craig felt himself climbing. The snow was thin here, the ground protected by hills rising abruptly behind the grubby mining camp. The paint drew up on a flat. To the right was a scatter of shacks and the lights of the Goldbar saloon. A good fifteen horses stood outside, stomping against the cold. Inside, Craig thought sourly, would be Luvain's hardcases, building their courage with cheap whiskey.

He turned left, toward the now whitened piles of mine tailings. A wide trail ran twistingly up the mountainside with branches going off to gaping holes in cliff faces or to small, dark shacks. Once this had obviously been a thriving mining community; now it was only an excuse for Luvain's men—a place where they could pretend to be making a living while they fattened themselves on valley beef.

He shook his head. From all he had heard, not enough cattle had been taken from the valley these past months to keep a small gang well fed, let alone a crew the size of Luvain's. Then how did they make their money? And as he worked his way up the slope, the snow thickening under the paint's hooves, he worked on the problem.

Someone had to be helping Luvain, paying him to do what he was doing. The answer struck Craig like a physical blow. There was only one man in the Sangaree with reason enough to want to break the ranchers, only one man with resources enough to afford to break them. And now Craig understood something that had puzzled him earlier—why Luvain and his men would have held a meeting in the dead-end gulch so many hours before they were due to make their hit—and then separate, some going to Goldbar to wait for time to make the attack, others going to town to get Marnie, and Luvain riding into the hills to set his trap.

No, it hadn't been Luvain and his men Anita Jerrod had

110

overheard, but Luvain and the man behind him. It had been Cloyd Luvain and Park Jerrod.

The road lifted abruptly over a rise and onto a narrow flat. The mines lay behind. Ahead was darkness, half of the glittering night sky blotted by the sheer, saw-toothed mountains reaching upward. Craig reined in the paint and turned his mind back to the immediate problem. He could see the faint line of the trail twisting down and out of sight— into the big canyon, he guessed. That meant the border could not be far away to the north.

Carefully, Craig edged the paint along the now narrow trail. It sloped gently at first and then more steeply as it angled down toward the canyon floor. But this was high country, even down in the canyon, and the snow was heavier here than Craig had met before. At first he cursed it, and then he realized that it was helping the paint, keeping it from plunging too quickly down what would be a treacherous slide under only a light coating of snow or ice.

On the valley floor, the snow became a handicap again for a time. The land was level here, having risen abruptly from the south. Craig studied the unbroken snow and then turned the paint in the general direction of the valley. He judged that he must be a good mile or better above the big rock where they had fought the rustlers. According to Anita's story, somewhere in that mile was a trap waiting for him.

As he reasoned, Luvain would be expecting him to ride up from below. That would mean a tired horse, fighting snow hock-high and therefore unable to maneuver at its rider's commands. And if Luvain was thinking this way, it could mean that he would be looking down-trail, waiting for the chance to spring his trap. Craig figured his chances of getting Marnie safely away were as good as doubled by his coming down into the trap from above.

The paint reached the steep downslope of this part of the canyon floor, and again the snow was an advantage. Craig studied the trail, noticing how the canyon narrowed here and broadened there, how it twisted almost back on itself in one place in its writhing upward climb.

There was no sound now but the gusty breathing of the paint. The wind had died away completely, leaving only the deadly stillness of deepening cold. The faint noise made by the paint breaking the soft snow pack was swallowed in the darkness. As he rode, Craig tried to hear what might lie ahead—to catch a flutter of voice, a clink of harness, a hint of someone waiting.

Then he heard it. To his right was the deeper blackness of an opening in the black face of the canyon wall. To his left was an outcropping of rock just big enough to hide a waiting man. The sound seemed to have come from his right, from the opening in the canyon wall.

Cautiously, gently, Craig slipped off a glove and eased his .44 into his hand. He angled the paint toward the dark blotch, his head swiveling at each step to make sure no one was crouched in the shadow by the rock overhang. But the single sound he had heard—the clink of rock on rock—was not repeated. He rode into the opening and stopped. Starlight showed him faintly that he was in a shallow topless cave, barely big enough to hide one horse and rider in the darkness.

He called softly, "Marnie?" and waited for some kind of answer, if only a faint, gagged moan. There was nothing. The sound had been a rock breaking from the cliff face from the cold, he thought disgustedly. Holstering his gun, he slid his hand back into his glove and returned to the trail.

He went around a final bend and saw the last slope before the canyon floor flattened out again. He could make out the dark bulk of the big rock shoulder. Puzzled, he slowed the paint. Anita Jerrod had said something about a side canyon, yet he had passed nothing but that large hollow in the rock face. He glanced in both directions. The canyon walls seemed smooth here.

He wondered if she had lied to him. He shook his head. More likely, Luvain had given her false information—as she had said, not trusting her. Craig started the paint on again.

From the darkness ahead, the heavy darkness at the base of the rock shoulder, a curse lifted in the air. Then a horse darted into the open, badly controlled, fighting snow that at this point had drifted almost belly-deep. The rider was small and strangely immobile.

112

It was Marnie, Craig saw, and he jerked off his glove and reached for his handgun. A deep laugh sounded from behind him, freezing his motion. Slowly he turned in the saddle. He stared upslope at the heavy bulk of Cloyd Luvain seated on his big smoke horse.

Luvain laughed again, and starlight winked faintly on the barrel of his carbine as he waggled it in Craig's direction. "You should have looked closer in that hollow, Craig. And you shouldn't have tried to outsmart me. I figured you might think about sneaking down from the top side."

Craig stared helplessly into the muzzle of the carbine, not twenty feet away. Luvain had been cleverer than he. Instead of his catching Luvain off guard, it was the other way around. And now he was helpless, his bare fingers half frozen to his gun butt, to a gun still buried in leather.

"All right," Craig said, "you've won this round, Luvain. But it won't do you any good."

Luvain cocked the carbine with a sharp sound. "It'll do my soul a lot of good to put a bullet in your belly—where it'll hurt the most and where you'll die slow. And all the time you're dying, think about the mistake you made tangling with Cloyd Luvain—and about the mistake you made murdering my brother."

Craig turned his back on Luvain and looked downslope. Marnie and her horse were close to him now and he could see that she was roped to the saddle in such a way that she could not move. The reins ran to her hands tied down to the saddle horn so that only by throwing her whole weight from side to side did she have any control over the horse at all. And now it was floundering in a deep drift. A gag stopped her from saying anything to him, Craig saw. But he was close enough to read her eyes—to see the hope that had flared there slowly dying away.

He twisted back to look upslope at Luvain. "What are you going to do with Miss Clayton?"

"Why," Luvain said in his thickest bayou drawl, "I was going to let the lady go back home. But one of my men got foolish and said a little too much where she could hear. So I reckon that she'll just have to stay here with you."

"If you're talking about Jerrod's part in all this," Craig

113

said, "you're too late to keep everyone in the Sangaree from knowing about it."

"Did you figure that out or did Anita tell you?" Luvain mocked.

Craig saw that his bluff had failed, that Luvain was actually going to have Marnie killed to keep her from telling what she knew. He stared beyond her, at the shadow by the rock shoulder. How many men were hiding there? At least two, perhaps three, he thought. It would have taken that many to subdue Clara and get Marnie away quietly.

His face stretched against the cold as he smiled at Marnie. Then, ignoring Luvain, he flattened himself in the saddle, kicked the paint forward and at an angle away from Marnie and drew his gun. He fired three times, raking the darkness by the butt of the rock shoulder before Luvain's gun cracked on the icy air, before he felt the impact of the bullet that lifted him half out of the saddle. Desperately he clung to his gun with one hand and to the saddle horn with the other. The paint snorting in terror, plunged straight for the dark base of the rock overhang. Craig shook his head to clear the mists of pain from his eyes.

And now he saw two riders coming at him, guns raised. Luvain behind, and Shorty with Jenks ahead, he thought. He made an effort to lift his gun but there seemed to be no strength in his arm. There was nothing here for him—ahead or behind—but death.

XVIII

CRAIG HEARD a wild curse rising on the air behind him. A gun went off and the curse came again, smothered suddenly. Shorty swung his gun away from Craig.

"It's that crazy female. She's ridden the boss into the snow. She'll have that horse trample him to death!"

Craig found the strength to turn as both men swept past him. He saw that somehow Marnie had managed to work her hands loose enough to handle the reins. She had apparently ridden her horse against Luvain's big gray as he sent it charging downslope toward Craig. And now Luvain was

114

down in the snow and Marnie was running her horse at him, making it slash at his crazily rolling body with its hooves.

Somewhere Craig found the strength to lift his gun. He fired just as Shorty drew his bead on Marnie. Shorty cried out as his gun was ripped from his hand, tearing the cold flesh. Jenks turned back to face Craig, and Craig shot him in the face. He fell forward across his saddle horn and his horse raced through the broken snow upslope and out of sight. Craig fired again, at Luvain, and missed.

With a last desperate effort, Luvain got to his feet, caught the stirrup of his big smoke and jerked himself erect and into the saddle. Craig cried, "Marnie! Here!" He lifted his gun to line it on Luvain, holding his fire until Marnie was beside him and then behind him.

Luvain, with that quickness of movement that always surprised Craig, had his own .44 in his hand and he snapped a shot at Marnie. It missed, whining off the rock shoulder behind her. Craig tried to answer and heard only the click of an empty gun.

"Get in the dark by the rock," Craig ordered Marnie. He jammed his .44 back in its holster and reached for his carbine. Luvain fired, but Craig was sawing the reins, making the paint dance, and the shot missed. Shorty continued to sit in the saddle, his bleeding hand clamped under his armpit, a steady stream of curses running from his mouth.

"Shut up and help me!" Luvain screamed at him. He fired again, but again, the dancing paint caused him to miss. Craig finally managed to free the carbine from its icy boot. The paint had carried him back into shadow alongside Marnie and he took his time lifting the gun, sighting on Luvain, peering now to find him against the dark face of the rock.

And then it was as if the carbine had turned to water and flowed out of Craig's hands. As if his whole body had become smoke and was drifting out of the saddle. He felt the rush of icy air and the chill impact of the snow, and he knew that he was struggling against its choking softness. But somehow he could do nothing and finally he only wanted to let himself sink down into it.

How long he lay unconscious, he was not sure, but he found himself on his knees, his hands digging into rough rock and pulling his body upright. He turned, propping his back against the wall of stone. Shots continued to ring in his ears and he shook his head, clearing haze from in front of his eyes and from his brain.

Luvain and Shorty were split, Luvain almost directly to Craig's left and Shorty part way up the slope of the canyon floor. Shorty had his carbine out and he was shooting wildly into the darkness where Craig stood. But his bullets were both high and wide as each move of his torn hand made his whole body jerk.

Luvain had only his handgun, and he was unable to keep the smoke horse still enough to draw a good bead with it. Marnie knelt close to Craig, half hidden behind a downed, motionless horse, and slowly, methodically, she drove carbine bullets at Luvain and then at Shorty, keeping both off balance and both at bay.

Craig dropped to his knees beside her and fumbled a load into his handgun. She said, not looking at him, "By the time I managed to work myself loose, you were coming to. But don't move much, Ben. You lost a lot of blood."

Craig could feel the sticky warmth of his own strength filling his boot, and for the first time he realized where he had been hit. Luvain's bullet had taken him across the top of the thigh, cutting a furrow through skin and muscle and going on out without touching bone.

"I'll be all right," he said, and his voice was thin in his own ears. He tried to steady the handgun and then had to rest his elbow on the flank of the dead horse to take his aim. He fired at Luvain, trying to judge the movements of the smoke. He swore silently as he saw that he missed the rider and instead ripped hide from the big animal's rump. The horse neighed in pain and leaped, carrying Luvain down trail, beyond their sight.

"There's two of them!" Shorty cried. "Boss, Craig's still alive!"

"The devil with Craig!" Luvain shouted back. "What can he do but bleed to death? There's no way out of this canyon but up to Goldbar or down to the valley. You go stand

116

guard up at the top. You can do that much. Biddle is still down below if he did like I said and stayed put. He can keep 'em from going that way." He laughed, a little wildly now, Craig thought.

"Me," Luvain cried, "I'm going down to get the boys started. By the time Craig dies, the woman won't be good for much. And if she does come crawling back, she won't find no place to go. Because I'm going to own it all!"

"Did you ask Jerrod about that?" Craig called mockingly.

Luvain cursed him. "Jerrod won't live any longer than you will, Craig." He laughed again. "Take your choice, *marshal*, bleed to death or freeze to death. It don't matter to me."

Marnie snapped a final shot at Shorty, but he was riding upslope, following the trail the other horses had broken, and was too far for accuracy. Soon he disappeared around a bend.

Craig said, "This horse?" and bent to see if it might be the paint.

"It belongs to the third man who was holding me," Marnie said. "Your first shots killed him and the horse both. Our two are safe."

She laid down the gun and turned toward Craig. "Lie up on the horse so I can look at your leg."

"There's a fresh shirt in my saddlebags," Craig said. "You can rip that up for bandages."

He was content for the moment to do as she told him and lie on the still slightly warm body of the animal while she cut away enough of his pantleg to make a pad and then wrap it with a sleeve of his fresh flannel shirt. As she worked, she told him briefly how Shorty, Jenks, and a third man she did not know had come to the restaurant and taken her at gunpoint, tying up Clara and pushing her in the pantry.

"They brought me here and roped me the way you saw," she went on. "Then when you came down the trail, Jenks shouted to pretend I was breaking loose and then he quirted my horse into the open."

"Luvain's trap almost worked," Craig said. "Almost, but not quite."

"It worked well enough," Marnie said bitterly. "We'll

117

have to find wood and build a fire to keep from freezing to death. And by the time we can find a way out of here, it will be too late. He'll have the valley."

"The ranchers are warned and Clara went to town to form a posse and bring them out," he said. "Luvain won't have it as easy as he thought."

Marnie said in her quiet way, "Does Clara know that Jerrod is behind Cloyd Luvain?"

"No, but Anita does. She—" He broke off. "She didn't say anything to me; she won't say anything to Clara," he said. "After all, Jerrod is her husband—I don't think she'll betray him or she would have before."

"And that means Clara will let Jerrod help her form the posse and he'll lead them to the valley," Marnie said.

Craig knew what she meant. Jerrod would lead the posse to anywhere else but the places where the fighting would be going on. He was clever enough to do it and make it look sensible. And by the time the townsmen arrived at the right place, it would be too late.

He knew he was judging things right when Marnie said, "I heard Luvain and his men talking. They've got another dozen hardcases from north of the border. He has an army of at least two dozen men!"

Craig lifted himself to his feet and tested his leg. It barely held his weight. "In that case," he said, "we've got to get out of here and warn the townsmen—now."

"How?" she demanded. "One man at each end can hold us in this canyon."

"We aren't going out the end," Craig answered. "We're going up the side." He pointed to the wall on their right. "We're going up there."

Locating the paint, he climbed awkwardly into the saddle. Making sure that he had both his .44 and his carbine and that Marnie had the dead man's carbine and his extra ammunition, Craig led the way to the spot where the tight, twisting little trail came steeply down to the canyon floor from above.

"Cardon took us in this way when we caught the rustlers," he explained. "If we got down, we can go back up."

"With all this snow!"

"Not too much stuck there," he pointed out. "It's too steep. You'll have to do the hard work." She listened while he explained his idea briefly. Then with a quiet nod, she left the saddle, took the reins of her horse and started walking up the trail.

The horse went reluctantly and now and then Marnie had to stop, turn, and brace herself with her bootheels while she pulled him up the steep, snow-covered stretches. Slowly, achingly, Craig saw her inch the animal up through the snow, breaking the crust, pawing down to solid ground beneath. And finally she was at the top and out of sight.

He remained where he was, wishing his leg had the strength to let him get off the paint and stomp some circulation into his numbed legs and feet. But he could only sit helplessly and endure the biting cold.

Finally Marnie reappeared, walking without the horse this time. Craig stepped awkwardly from the saddle. He took his rope and the one from the dead horse. Using the saddle blanket off the dead animal, he rigged a cradle with the ropes, hooking their ends to the sides of his own saddle. When he lay down on the blanket-cradle, he was separated by a good ten feet from the paint's rear hooves. Even so, he knew, he would get hard balls of snow in his face.

"All right," he said to Marnie. "Lead him off."

"Stay on your back," she said pleadingly. "If you fall on that wound and open it again . . ."

"I may lose the seat of my britches," Craig said lightly, "but I promise to keep your bandage on tight."

Marnie managed a shaky laugh. Then she took the reins of the paint and started up the sleep slope. Lying on his back behind, Craig shouted at the horse, his familiar voice making it dig in and fight its way up the slope instead of balking as the other horse had done.

It was a strange ride and one he had no urge to repeat. With ten feet of taut but flexible rope between himself and the paint, Craig was bounced helplessly in his cradle. As the paint took a sharp switchback, the blanket slid toward the outer edge of the trail and, once, only by throwing his weight wildly inward did he manage to keep from being hurtled off the edge. Underneath him, the chewed snow had already begun to crust over and now and then a jagged piece of ice-like snow ripped through the blanket and his clothes and dug into his skin.

When the paint topped the last rise and stopped, legs spraddled and head drooping, Craig crawled onto his knees and looked back down. The bottom of the canyon was lost in darkness.

He said, "There were times when I wasn't sure we'd make it."

Marnie had little breath or strength left, but she found enough to lift him to his feet. They stood a moment, staring into one another's faces. Then he dipped his head and found her lips with his. For a time there was no cold, no fight, nothing but the two of them in a silent, white world.

Marnie stepped back gently. "This is a strange time to get my first kiss," she said.

Craig turned to the paint. "I'm going now to make sure it isn't the last," he said. "Can you cut that blanket loose?"

Mounted, they rode the snow-covered trail toward the valley, going slowly until both horses had their wind back. Marnie laughed once, softly. And when he glanced inquiringly at her, she said, "In one breath, you hint that you love me. In the next, you give me a practical order."

He grinned with facial muscles stiff from cold. "After this is finished, it'll be different. Then we can forget the practical for a time."

"Are you proposing, sir?"

"I am," he said.

She murmured, "I wonder how many women have been proposed to on their way to a gunfight?"

Their half serious, half bantering talk helped take the curse off the cold and the weary miles. Then, as they neared the valley, the rumbling, persistent sound of gunfire brought them back to the ugly reality that lay ahead.

Craig reined in at the top of the last stretch of trail. The valley lay directly below. It was dark except for one great glow south and east that marked a burning haystack. But little pricks of light showed here and there as men fired at one another, and the chill air carried the sounds up to where Craig and Marnie rested.

Craig studied the scene for some time before he said, "There isn't much fighting going on around the ranchers' houses yet. If I know Luvain, he's planning to do more than just burn a few haystacks."

He paused again. "You know this country. If you were Jerrod and you were leading a posse of untrained fighters out here to help the ranchers, but you really wanted to keep them out of the fighting as long as possible, where would you take them?"

Marnie answered so quickly that he knew she had been thinking of this already. "I'd lead them as far west in the valley as I could. I'd probably tell them they were needed most to defend the houses and barns. And then when I couldn't hold them any longer, I'd try to signal Luvain to shift his attack from the hayfields to the houses and at the same time swing my posse over east, telling them we were going to make a pincer movement on Luvain and catch him between our fire and the ranchers'."

Craig grinned with his stiff facial muscles. "You'd make a good general."

"The problem isn't much harder than trying to design a stylish dress for some of the local women," she said dryly.

Craig chuckled and started the paint downslope. Once on the valley floor, he hesitated. "I don't like to see you getting this close to the fighting. If Jerrod is where we think, there could be trouble."

"And if he isn't where we think he is, you're going to need help finding him," she retorted. "He knows this country; you don't."

Craig's nod was an admission of agreement. He started off again, keeping tight to the edge of the west hills. They crossed Kearney Creek and he knew that they would meet Jerrod soon—or lose precious time trying to find him.

XIX

THEY WERE well below the fighting now, and the lights of town were brighter than the burning haystack or the pricks of light that marked guns firing. At this distance

121

from the fighting, the only sounds were made by the hooves of their horses breaking through the thin crust that had formed on the snow.

Another fifteen minutes, Craig thought, and they would be too far south—and that would mean Jerrod had done the unexpected and managed to take the posse even farther away from the action. Then he heard the jangle of harness and a muffled voice hissing for quiet.

The sound came from west of where he rode. Marnie drew alongside. "Jerrod has them on the hillslope," she whispered. "That means they can't have made much speed since they left town."

Craig's nod was lost in the darkness. He reined his paint to the right. "Lay back," he whispered. "This might not be Jerrod at all." He added, "If it is, don't expose him to the townsmen—not yet. Follow my lead."

Marnie ignored him and spurred ahead. Swearing softly, he followed at her heels. He heard someone on the slope ahead call out. Then he realized what she was doing as she swung her horse under an overhang that could protect them from a nervous shot fired from above.

"Someone's riding down there!" It was Briggs' rusty voice.

Craig called up, "Briggs! It's Craig here. Miss Clayton is with me."

Someone let out a cheer that was quickly muffled. Jerrod said, "Thank God! But what about Luvain?"

"He got away," Craig said. "He's shifted his attack and thrown his weight against the hayfields. I saw one go up already. And he has a good two dozen hardcases with him."

Riding into the open, Craig started the paint angling up the gentle slope here. He saw the dark blotch marking the posse and he had to admire Jerrod's nerve. The man had kept them far enough down the hill slope to make it appear as if they were riding far enough from any possible attackers around the ranch houses to keep from being easily heard, and at the same time he had chosen a route across rough land so that they could make little time reaching the scene of action.

Craig drew up near Jerrod, close enough to see that

122

the man had a carbine across his saddle bow and that it was pointed in his general direction.

"Our best chance to help is to ride straight east from here," Craig said, "and then come at Luvain from the rear. We can squeeze him between us and the ranchers if we move fast enough."

"Let's ride, then!" Briggs cried. And with surprising ability, the tubby little man sent his horse down the snow-covered slope and onto the flat of the valley. A good fifteen men followed him. Craig went more slowly with Jerrod staying behind and slightly to his left.

They reached the valley floor near the overhang. Craig said, "It was a clever trick, Jerrod, but it wouldn't have done you any good if it had worked."

"What the devil are you talking about?" Jerrod demanded.

"You and Luvain," Craig answered. "I figured it out for myself. But I needn't have bothered. Some of Luvain's men got loose jaws when Marnie was with them."

Jerrod swore and his carbine lifted. From behind him, Marnie said out of the darkness of the overhang, "I wouldn't, Mr. Jerrod. As Ben said, you can't win, no matter what you do."

Jerrod's gun muzzle dropped. Then he pushed the carbine into its boot and sat with his hands on the saddle horn. "What does that mean?"

"It means Luvain figures on killing you as soon as he takes over the valley," Craig said flatly. "He wants to own it all—valley, town, everything you have." He paused and added slowly, almost reluctantly, "Including your wife."

"That trash!"

"He's South and so is she," Craig said. "And if he were the only man around with money—her money included—and if he had the sense to pay her some of the attention a handsome woman likes, what do you think she'd do?"

The slump of Jerrod's shoulders was answer enough. Then he straightened. "You didn't tell what you knew about me and Luvain to the townsmen," he said. "Why not?"

"Let them fight first," Craig said. "They've got problems enough keeping their courage without worrying about seeing one of their idols smashed."

123

"Keep it that way until it's over," Jerrod said. It was typical, a command not a request. "Because I want Luvain for myself. I'll fight with you until this is ended, Craig. After that, it's each man for himself."

"Fair enough," Craig said. He turned to Marnie. "I expect Clara would like to see you and know you're safe."

Jerrod laughed abruptly. "More than that. She could use the help. She not only tongue-lashed fifteen townsmen into riding against Luvain, she's got the women and the old-timers armed and waiting in case Luvain wins. She has Fitchen to help but she'll need you too."

"All right," Marnie said. She sounded suddenly achingly weary. "Ben, your leg . . . ?"

"It's too cold to know the difference," Craig said. She rode off and he motioned Jerrod to go in front of him. "If we angle toward the near east corner of Kearney's place, we can catch up with the posse," he pointed out.

"We need to," Jerrod said in his clipped way. "None of them know the east hills well enough to use them to sneak down on Luvain. I do."

He was right, Craig learned. They caught the posse within a mile. Then, with Jerrod in the lead, they rode the east slopes through the shadow of scrub timber, over ground surprisingly free of the crusty snow. As they neared the place that was the obvious heart of the fighting, the crack of guns was an almost steady beat against the dark night. A second haystack had been fired, and the flames cast a great glow over a wide area, now and then showing up a horse and rider trying to maneuver.

With the fire in front of Luvain and his men, Craig saw their positions without too much trouble as one or another led a foray from the timber. They would cross the road at an angle, raking the defenders' positions with fire and then charge back into the darkness.

Jerrod said, "I haven't seen Luvain ride out yet. He must be planning something—picking away like this isn't his way of fighting."

"A flanker movement," Craig guessed. "He's smart. He'll keep the ranchers' attention with those charges from a half dozen men and when the time is right lead the rest north and then west and try to come in from behind."

"If he hasn't done it already," Briggs said, coming up closer.

"No," Craig said. "There isn't enough answering fire. That means the ranchers aren't all bunched here yet. They most likely suspect a trick. But if it doesn't come after a while, they'll probably figure a direct big hit will be made head-on and then they'll all pull into one place. That's when Luvain will make his move."

He paused and studied the situation. Ahead of them Luvain and his men were protected by clusters of thick scrub pines and by chopped up land that ran very close to the road here. The burning haystack was a bit north; the smoldering remains of the first one lay a little south. Roofed, open-sided feeding pens as well as the remaining haystacks gave the ranchers their only protection. If Luvain ever did manage to trick them into facing in one direction, he could cut their strength to ribbons.

"Leave about six men here," Craig told Briggs. "Then you and Jerrod take the rest and swing up above where Luvain is and work your way back down close to the road some distance north. But don't let yourselves be seen. And hold there until Luvain makes his attack."

"If he does," Jerrod said. "It's a cold night to be sitting."

"He won't sit long," Craig said. "I'm going to see that he attacks—and does it quick." He glanced back at the men, noting with surprise that some of those who had been least eager to defend the town that first night were well up in front now. Clara's tongue had a sharper edge than he'd thought.

He said, "Wallace, you and Teazel pick four other men and hold this position. If Luvain's crew tries to break south, you'll be waiting for them."

"And you?" Briggs asked rustily.

"I'm going down and have a talk with the ranchers," Craig said. "They're going to make the move that gets Luvain started on his trick. When he moves, light a match."

"For God's sake, don't get shot for one of Luvain's men," Briggs cautioned.

125

"Why worry? You'll make a fine marshal," Craig said, and then he rode away, out of range of Briggs' disgusted cursing.

But Briggs was right, he knew, and he wasted precious minutes backtracking the tired paint until he was far enough into the valley to ride toward the ranchers without being an easy target. There was no firing at all from the direction of the houses, and he guessed that Luvain's men had finished their diversionary maneuver there and had swung back to rejoin the main group.

He heard the crackle of hooves on crusted snow and called quickly at the heavy dark, "Craig here. Who is it?"

A deep grunt answered him and then Kearney's heavy voice. "We thought you were dead, marshal." He came close, swinging his gun aside as he recognized Craig. "I was riding to the house to tell the men there to sit tight—in case Luvain breaks through."

"Have you lost anybody yet?" Craig asked.

"One down and out of the fight and Finch has a bad left arm—but not as bad as that leg of yours from the looks of it. We got two of theirs dead in our sights. Otherwise, it's been mostly a waste of lead." He grunted again. "This isn't like Luvain, fighting in little hits."

Craig told him quickly of his idea and of the plan to use the posse. Kearney swore in surprise. "The townsmen came to help us !"

"You and themselves," Craig said.

"And you think they'll fight when things get a little hot—if we trick Luvain into trying his pincer maneuver?"

"If they don't fight, it won't matter what Luvain does," Craig said. "He's got close to two dozen men left. He can take you head-on or from the side sooner or later."

"All right. Let's talk to the others." Kearney swung his horse and trotted toward a clump of deep shadow cast by a large feeding pen with a huge stack of hay close beside it. Craig followed.

As he drew near, he could see the men guarding the attacks from the road. He counted only four. And there were six whole men and Finch at the feeding pen. "Is this all the crew you have?

"Truesdale is guarding the houses and barns with the rest of them," Kearney explained. Quickly, he told the men of Craig's idea.

"If the townsmen fight, we'll have 'em!" Tip Fraley exulted.

"I'm sure Luvain thinks there are more of you here," Craig said. "So we'll trick him another way too. Ride out in two groups—four at a time—taking a way that you can be seen from the road. Act as if you're making for the haystacks where those other men are. Then swing into the dark and come back here and make a second trip. That way, he'll count each of us twice. Then after the second swing through, we meet here—and wait for Luvain to move."

"You fought your share of Indians, all right," Finch said.

They broke into groups, Kearney leading the first, Craig with Finch in the second. The route took them across a good fifty feet of open space and they pressed their horses hard as lead from across the road whipped at them. In the two runs, one horse took a bullet across the rump, nearly unseating Tip Fraley, its rider, and Arty Logan lost his hat.

"Watch for a match flicker up in the hills," Craig said. "That will be Briggs' signal that Luvain is on the move. Then we wait until he crosses the road."

"He'd better hurry," Finch grumbled. "If they hadn't fired some of our hay, we'd have frozen to death before now."

It was a thin joke at best but it helped relieve the tension. Craig rode to where he could watch the slopes behind and a bit north of where Luvain and his men waited. He saw the quick flicker of light.

"They're moving!"

They lined up, eight men abreast, holding their horses quiet, listening for the telltale crackle of snow under racing hooves. It came more suddenly than they had expected. And now they could see the wave of riders—dark against darkness—sweeping across the road and angling toward them.

"Hold it," Craig snapped as Kearney lifted his gun.

Then he made out the townsmen coming down to the road, crossing it. "Now!" he ordered.

Eight carbines cracked, sending lead whining into the dark. A man cried in pain. Another cursed as he was lifted from the saddle. A horse neighed shrilly and turned, twisting into the animals behind him. And then, from behind, the townsmen opened their fire.

"Fall back," Craig said, "or our own posse will hit us."

They dropped back to the protection of the feed pen. Luvain began to shout, trying to hold his men as both sides poured fire into them. But the attack had been too sudden, too unexpected, and they broke, scattering across the valley floor. The posse's fire for the most part was wasted lead, but the ranchers fired with deadly accuracy, driving men out of their saddles, sending others racing in panic westward. And then others riders appeared, coming from the direction of the houses.

"That'll be Truesdale and the hill men!" Kearney cried. "By God, they'll cut every one of those hardcases down."

Not everyone, Craig thought. Because he could see the big bulk of Cloyd Luvain swing away from the fighting and race north and west. Almost at the same time, a slighter form detached itself from the townsmen and raced in pursuit. Jerrod!

Craig said, "I'm going after Luvain," and kicked the tired paint to life. The horse leaped forward. Craig reined it right toward the road, keeping clear of the shooting at the cost of precious distance. Once the road was under his feet, he raced northward, his eyes on Luvain and Jerrod in a grim race for the nearest place a man could make a stand—the thick willows along one of the creeks cutting across the valley floor.

Now Craig angled toward them. He saw Luvain swallowed by the darkness of the trees, saw Jerrod pull up and start a wide swing. A gun blasted from the trees, cutting Jerrod's horse down. Jerrod leaped from the saddle and bellied down, answering the fire with three quick shots. Craig changed his angle, crossing the creek well to the east of the shooting and then following it westward toward the sharp sounds of gunfire.

He pulled up the paint and dropped from the saddle. But his leg refused to hold him and awkwardly, he drew

128

himself back aboard the tired horse. He rode slowly now, his eyes seeking movement in the darkness cast by the trees.

There was a break in the screen of willows and through it he saw Jerrod rise up suddenly, fire into the air and then fall to the ground. He rolled over once and lay with his hands reaching toward Cloyd Luvain.

Luvain appeared on his gray smoke, not a dozen feet from where Craig sat the paint. He was laughing and talking to his horse. "Now we can take it easy, boy. And someday I'll come back and finish what I started here tonight."

"You're not riding anywhere, Luvain," Craig answered softly.

Luvain turned in the saddle. His gun was back in its holster. He held only the reins in his big hands. "Craig, by God!"

"That's right. And taking care of the rest of my promise to Chalco—right now. Draw, Luvain. And you'd better make it fast."

"And as soon as I twitch, you'll shoot."

"My gun's in its holster the same as yours."

Luvain laughed again, a thick sound this time. "But you ain't the type to shoot unless I do draw. So if I don't, what are you going to do, Craig?"

"Run you to town and let them hang you," Craig said evenly. "This way you have a chance."

He knew Luvain too well to concentrate on the man's words. His eyes were fixed on Luvain's shoulder. He saw the first imperceptible dip of it, the first warning of Luvain's draw. Then Luvain's hand blurred to his hip and came up holding his .44. Craig's own gun was out before Luvain finished clearing leather. He let Luvain line up his shot and then fired. The bullet caught Luvain in the face, sending him backward off the gray horse. He lay in the snow, not moving.

Craig said thickly to the paint, "I'll ride the smoke and give you a rest, fellow." When he stepped out of the saddle, he kept going forward until he lay stretched out, as unmoving as Luvain.

It was the warmest snow Craig had ever felt. He opened

his eyes and stared in surprise at the faces peering down at him. He saw Doctor Yates and a worried looking Briggs. Then behind them, Marnie appeared and came to him.

"Thank heaven Briggs had the sense to go after you," she said. "That was a crazy thing to do!"

"Not as crazy as what I'm going to do," Craig said, "as soon as all this riffraff gets out of here."

Doc Yates said sourly, "He'll live." He started for the door. "Well, come on, Briggs, you've only got a few days more to be marshal. Then he'll be up and around again."

Craig laughed and the sound felt good, loose and free inside. "No," he said. "Not a few days—as long as you want. I'm riding out when I'm well.".

"I—I . . ." Briggs said. But for once he could think of nothing to say. He left with the doctor.

"So you really are leaving," Marnie murmured.

"With my wife," Craig said. He recalled something Clara had once said. "We can live close to Portland and you can set up a fancy dress place and I'll breed horses. My brother can run the cattle ranch the way he has been. We'll do fine."

The door opened and Clara came in. "I heard that. I heard everything but you asking her to marry you."

"He did that the other night," Marnie said.

"And you accepted?"

"I guess I did," she answered. "He sounds as if I did, doesn't he?"

Craig laughed again and drew her face down to his. When the kiss ended, he lifted his head. "Clara, you'll be coming with us?"

"Not on your tintype, I won't!" she snapped. "I'm going to run the Sangaree House—and see that the men in this town get a little decent food now and then."

"What about Mrs. Jerrod?"

But Clara was gone. Marnie said, "She sold a lot and paid all the people back whose money had been taken from the bank. She still owns the ranch and the hotel and some of the stores. She's going back down South and live off the rent money they bring."

"Fine," Craig said. "But are you sure Clara wants to stay here alone—or is she just helping Anita Jerrod out?"

"According to Clara," Marnie said with a perfectly straight face, "there are a few widowers in town who showed enough gumption the other night to make themselves worth her notice. Don't worry about her being alone, Ben."

He reached for her again. "I won't worry about Clara," he murmured. "But I'll do a heap of worrying about those widowers."

Louis Trimble was born in Seattle, Washington, and during most of his professional career taught in the University of Washington system of higher education. 'I began writing Western fiction,' he later observed, 'because of my interest in the history and physical character of the western United States and because the Western was (and is) a genre in which a writer could move with a great deal of freedom.' His first Western novel under the Louis Trimble byline was *Valley of Violence* (1948). In this and his subsequent Western novels he seems to have been most influenced by Ernest Haycox, another author who lived in the Pacific Northwest. He also used the *nom de plume* **Stuart Brock** under which he wrote five exceptional Westerns, all published by Avalon Books in the 1950s. The point of focus in his Western fiction, whether he is writing as Louis Trimble or Stuart Brock, constantly shifts among various viewpoints and women are often major characters. *Railtown Sheriff* (1949) was Trimble's first Western novel as Stuart Brock and it was under this byline that some of his most exceptional work appeared, most notably *Action at Boundary Peak* and *Whispering Canyon*, both in 1955, and *Forbidden Range* in 1956. These novels have strong characters, complex and realistic situations truly reflecting American life on the frontier, and often there is a mystery element that heightens a reader's interest. The terrain of the physical settings in these stories is vividly evoked and is an essential ingredient in the narrative. Following his retirement from academic work, Trimble made his retirement home in Devon, England.